Sisters

PIECED
TOGETHER

Sisters

PIECED

TOGETHER

Névine Zariffa

To my sisters

The one I grew up with, and the ones I met along the way

You walk with me as I do with you

Contents

Chapter 1

Coping with the Sun

I met Francine the day we buried my sister. That Saturday was a perversely bright, sunny day. Susie's light had gone out and a cloak of grief enveloped those of us who remained. I couldn't manage the sun; my mind was in the shadows where dimness prevailed. I didn't realize until months later that Francine set in motion that day an elaborate play, much better than anything I could have written. She stood at a small gravestone several rows away from my twin sister's more elaborate burial place, the place I would come to often. At first, Susie called me there. Soon it would be Francine.

It was hard not to notice Francine. She wore a large black hat, stylish in that old-world European fashion. No American would ever wear something like that, at least no one I knew. The hat did an excellent job of protecting her from the sun, though the nearby willow tree would have done better. I guessed she was sixty or seventy. Her bright red lipstick had faded because she was outside for most of the afternoon. She had small black eyes and a pixie face of a long-ago elegance.

The rest of her outfit matched her hat perfectly. A classic black suit. Could it be a Chanel? The purse certainly was, or a good knockoff. I knew these things from Susie, who was a clotheshorse. Had been. Tenses were tricky for me for a while.

But her elegance is not all that I noticed. She was watching me. I tried to avoid being distracted. I was there to talk to Susie, to try to connect with her even though she was gone. I was left with my guilt and the weight of events that led me here. Could Susie still hear me now as I whispered my confession? I spoke ever more softly so the woman in black couldn't hear. So softly, I eventually stopped moving my lips. Could my twin sister still read my mind?

It was hard not to watch Francine as she turned to leave. She wore light-colored one-inch heels that dug into the cemetery ground with every step. I could see she had slim ankles and a good turn of the leg. Maybe a dancer? She nodded at me as she walked away, leaving behind a waft of light perfume. I recognized it as female power, the delicate version. Easy to underestimate.

It was the only time that day I thought of anything other than Susie's death and the part I played in it.

$$\infty$$

"JK, there you are. Your mother has been looking for you. She's in the kitchen." It was my father speaking softly, overwhelmed by the loss of Susie. Dad was a good guy by all accounts. I hugged him, but not too hard. He was fragile.

"Dad. Yeah, sorry. I needed some time to myself." A paltry excuse by any standard. I was always the lesser sibling—five years in and out of rehab while Susie was a star in medical school. Dad never tried to pretend otherwise. Mom was another story. She was a fighter and wanted more from me, no matter what.

I wasn't in the kitchen long. The smell of the food made me sick. My empty stomach should have had me pick up a plate of food so I could feed it, but it was no good trying to convince me of anything. I had been going on hazy instincts all day. Mom nodded at me across the island just before I left.

I headed out to the living room, where the fine people close to our lives assembled to pay their respects. We lived in one of Palo Alto's best neighborhoods. The houses were not too big and close to each other. It created a community. Men and women in your business, in the kindest possible way, over the hedges of the small, manicured gardens. When Susie and I left for college, Mom kept the neighbors updated on our lives as she tended her plantings. These people knew a lot about us. I am sure Mom edited my life heavily . . . but not Susie's, golden child with golden hair.

Mrs. Summers got hold of me first in the hallway. "Dear, we are all so sorry about your sister. She was *so* very young." Her tired face peered into mine. She held out her hand to touch my face, but she pulled it back before it made contact. I squeezed her arm and moved on to the living room, where there were more sympathies to acknowledge.

"It is *so* terrible."

"I'm *so* sad when I think of it."

"It's *so* awful. I mean that."

"A tragedy, such a tragedy."

At least someone wasn't using the word *so*.

Before long, I found a spot on my folks' ugly green couch, a 1960s heirloom they never replaced. The mourners came to me then, and it wasn't as easy to get away from the well-intentioned crowd. But at least my back didn't hurt from standing, and the haziness of the day stopped hovering around me. It too sat down.

I tuned out the clumsy attempts at comfort from those hovering above me. Dismissed by my silence, they turned to chitchat in low voices to more receptive ears. People showered me with their feelings about Susie. It suited me just fine; I didn't want to share any of my feelings with these folks. The worst ones seemed to thrive on this type of thing as if our family's misery was their chance to shine. I had dark thoughts.

"JK. I've been looking for you." And there she was, The Mother. The woman who had given birth to Susie and me. We were fraternal twins, Susie and me. We looked nothing alike, of course. Nor did we do anything the same way. But we were close, the way only cells dividing alongside each other in that swimming pool called the womb can be.

Mom sat next to me. The couch sagged a little under our weight. We became the two-for-one deal. Mourners rushed at us both. I couldn't have shielded her if I had tried. Mom was tough and more experienced than I was about social gatherings. She was almost gracious about the inane comments. I stayed quiet.

Later that night, I came to understand that my mother—Susie's mother that day—harbored a secret. We were putting away the food in the Tupperware produced from all corners of my mother's well-stocked kitchen when she unburdened herself. Beyond the simple language of putting things away, Mom finally spoke. "At least Susie's suffering stopped."

My mother was fierce in all things. At least I thought so until those words. I looked up in surprise from the pot roast I had been packing up. She had been nothing but a battle-hungry warrior in the hospital, threatening to take Susie to a better place if they could not offer her a reasonable prognosis.

Towards the end, she even scolded the young volunteer in charge of books about the sheets' cleanliness. Mom's chipped manicured nails pointed to Susie's hospital bed while she railed about the stains "on the bed linen." That young girl had come to offer solace not knowing we could not be consoled. Instead, we taught her about human nature that day. Her nametag said Georgina. That's an old-fashioned name for a thirteen-year-old. Lucky for Georgina, she wasn't alone; and the older do-gooder took her out of Susie's room. Away from the mother. Away from the drama. Over to another room where the sick and dying behaved better.

"Mom?"

"I know. But there it is, JK. There it is."

She was at the sink, her tears falling into the soapy water. My Amazon of a mother, undone. Wait—weren't they virgins, the Amazons? Maybe that is why I never thought that moment was real. My mother would never wish her child dead, nor would she cry.

In that moment's fantasy, I placed my hand on her back; hiccups racked her body when she started to sob. She shook her head and dropped the sponge into the soapy water, where it made more of a splash than her tears. None of it was real. What to do next? My feet shuffled right and left. I was not up to the task.

I left Mom alone in the kitchen. Dad was cleaning out the living room. He would comfort her, I thought. Isn't that what husbands do for their wives? I rarely thought of my parents as a couple; Susie brought up that kind of thing.

When she was doing chemo and was half bald, Susie had asked me, "Do you think they have sex?"

"Ugh! Get away from me, you pervert!" I shoved her playfully.

But Susie was tough. Strong and determined like Mom. She just had other battles to fight. She came right back at me. "No, really, do you think they still do? They're pretty old now. I bet Mom is the one who decides either way."

Imagine a thirty-year-old doctor in a chemo chair asking her twin such a question. I guess those drippy-type drugs make you crazy. Duly qualified doctors might have prescribed them, but they worked the same as the drugs I had once taken from street dealers. The truth was I had not thought about Mom and Dad as human beings in a while. Susie, as always, was ahead of me.

That first night ceremonially confirmed us as being a family without Susie. "Family" was a big word for us at this point. Dad turned away from the kitchen and walked into his study. I knew he would sleep in there. It seemed to me my parents might never touch each other again. I had no one in my life. No touching hands for me, soothing, sexy, or depraved. I had all three versions in the past. Now it was a desert.

I walked up the small flight of stairs where my and Susie's pictures played along and accompanied me. Milestones of all kinds were up on that wall. Our braces, shows, Halloween costumes, candid shots, and graduation formal portraits were a riot of happiness. Stop smiling, foolish girls.

My leg muscles clenched in sympathy with my fist.

My sister was dead. Picture that.

The following day, I woke up late with no parents in sight. I headed straight back to the cemetery. The sign at the entrance said Memorial Garden. The manager had explained to my parents that everyone was welcome there. I had not asked whether the woman was talking about the living or the dead. Susie's new place was a cemetery. The brochure could not dress it up any different. It was within walking distance of my parents' house, but I rode the bus that day.

That sun from the day before was still there. I could only see it as a burden, compelling me to a brighter world than I could handle. I stood at the cemetery gates. Stuck in my thoughts. I was too petrified to move towards the dead. My feelings gnarled around my mind and rooted me to the ground.

My sister was dead, and I was paralyzed by it.

I saw the black hat coming towards me, the woman stepping through the main path on her way out. I took a few steps sideways, avoiding the giant pothole in the driveway. Not the best cemetery, though it's even worse when they're pristine and precious.

"Are you bitter?" The woman in the hat said as she stopped next to me.

"Uh, that's an awkward question."

It was the best I could do with no coffee and no bagel that morning. I'm usually much wittier, also known as a smart ass.

The hat came back at me. "Quite so, and yet it seems like the question to ask."

My mind was blank, or rather overfull. Thoughts raced despite my numbness. She waited for a while for me to respond. When no answer came, she walked away with grit on her heels. My mind was suddenly quiet as I watched her figure recede. My only thought was that she had dirtied her shoes.

I stood battling the sun's brightness at the cemetery's

threshold and wondered about bitterness. There was something theatrical about the woman in the black hat. Also something enticing. Theatrics were close to my heart. I was a writer; well, more correctly, a has-been / wannabe writer. "Aspiring" and "washed up" all at once.

An eager producer, himself in a slump, snapped up the first screenplay I wrote. My Berkeley professor had shared my play with him as soon as my copyright deposit was acknowledged. The old guy looked out for me as much as he could, but the producer ate me alive anyway. Dear professor Smithfield was a little out of his league outside the walls of higher education.

You probably hear that Hollywood is tough. Well, it's the people in Hollywood who are demanding—and selfish. For a while, I was one of them. I graduated from selfish to self-centered somewhere along the way. Then, I got evicted from the fold. And now I was "at-large," just plain lost.

My work reflected what I saw in the mirror every morning after I finished putting on my getup. My writing had no depth. But it shocked the yuppies alright. It was "novel," "bold," "unexpected," so the critics said. For a while, my stories about punk kids roaming wild did well.

I was hysterical. Success does that to the unprepared. Or is it the adulation? The purposeful compliments from hard-nosed professionals turned my head right around. Hollywood dropped my hard-edge, smart-as-a-whip, sassy series after one season. I got calls for about a year. The problem was I was dried out, cruising the highway at top speed, going nowhere. Life was—well, it was. It's pretty sad to be a washout at twenty-four. I sank down for a couple more years, as if taking the drop to the bottom were some great journey. How small can a person get? It was Susie who came to help me. My sister.

Yeah, I hated the sun.

It was time for some caffeine to clear my mind. I found myself in a Dunkin Donuts shop you see everywhere now. Back then, the solitary California franchise had not yet caught on widely across the state. Susie introduced me to it when I visited her at college.

After two cups of the home brew and several bagels, I stared out the window, debating my next move. The sun was now high in the sky; I would not cast a shadow if I headed out. Susie was waiting for me. I had to go. The DD's double comfort of food and drink had done its thing. I acknowledged the contribution and walked straight over to Susie's grey granite headstone.

"Hey, Susie. It's me, JK."

I had beaten the sun and its bright rays washing away the city grime—no small victory. I was, however, failing at talking to the stone, no better at that than writing. I tried, though. I tried for Susie.

"Hey, Sis. Hiya. They all came out for you. Did you hear what people said? Yeah, all good. Not as good as you deserve, but good. You were the star, babe. I know how much you like that, even if you say you don't."

"Right, no teasing. I promise. Well, make that I'll try. I know how

picky you are with words. Gosh, you should have been the writer."

"I keep wondering where you are. Did you see us yesterday? Maybe you have better things to do."

"Is … is the pain … is it really gone? Mom thinks it is, you know."

"I hope you know it's pretty crappy out here without you."

"Me? Oh, I am getting used to the sun again."

Later. *"OK. Well, then, see ya, Sis."*

Much later. *"I miss you."*

I walked away from Susie. It hurt like a bitch—again. Repetition at its best. The sun had come down quite a bit, and it might even have been chilly. I couldn't tell anymore. I'd have to try for a better conversation with Susie. That one was lame, just like the last scripts I wrote. There was more at stake now. I really should suck it up.

As I passed the gate, a question stole into my thoughts. That woman in the black hat. What was her accent? French? Maybe. I'd have to find out. If I saw her again.

"So, JK. Have you thought about how long you're going to stay?"

It was my dad's way of starting a conversation. Usually, before Susie left us, that is, I ignored these overtures. But I didn't have the heart for that now. His eyes were filled with sadness. Susie would have wanted me to talk with him. She always wanted us to get along as a family. Susie was our mascot and cheerleader all in one. She looked the part: pert, pretty, all-American, blonde, blue-eyed. Susie was the gal next door but with steel underneath that attractive package.

I was the opposite with my rebel look. I made things uncomfortable for everybody after I sank into my pit of failure. I wore my distress visibly: perforations, brown hair turned to black, greasy eyeliner, dark lipstick. My transformation began in college. The drop to the basement post-Hollywood accelerated the change from edgy to grungy. Mom twitched at my clothes, but she focused on the bigger issues. Why, why, after a perfect childhood, could I not cope with a minor setback? Dad never judged. Susie, my anchor, would defend me.

"Dunno, Dad. I thought I might stay a while. If that's okay with you and Mom."

Was Susie smiling even a little?

"JK, that would be great, just great. We'd love to have you here."

I couldn't help but grin. Dad looked almost happy for the first time in months. Just like that, at the thought of having JK around for a while. Susie would be relieved to see us together.

"I'll get us a couple of beers. You still have the non-alcoholic ones, right?"

"Of course, JK, that's all we keep now. I'll be out on the porch."

The neighbors walked past. Without a formula to dictate

their sympathies, they put up a hand or nodded at us. We were out of the social fabric, at least for a while. I don't think Dad minded at all. Not one bit. I know I didn't.

It was after the second set of beers that Dad finally said what was on his mind.

"It wasn't your fault, you know. That's just how things turned out. Susie loved you something fierce."

Dad, who had once been such a great big guy to us, added rather shyly, "We all love you, JK. All of us."

I was stunned. Dad never spoke about his feelings. Susie and I used to wonder about that. Funny, she never asked me why I kept my feelings to myself. She accepted my acerbic wit as the substitute, even as we debated Dad's great wall of silence.

For once, the smart ass under my costume kept its mouth shut. It was some version of Susie who spoke, using my voice: "I hear you. I hear you alright, Dad."

Mom came out then, the screen door squeaking. She took one look at us and went back into the house. Another door squeaked. Dad and I finished our beers and went back inside. There were sandwiches on the dining room table. Just two of them, with two empty glasses next to the plates and two paper napkins. But no napkin rings. Mom was some of the way back to her usual self. Fair enough. Who knew how to get back to normal anyway?

There was not much more to say. Mom was back upstairs in her bedroom, door shut tight as a drum. No need for the "Do not enter" sign that once adorned my teenage door.

Nope, it would not be easy.

I helped Dad set up the old cot we used for cousins sleeping over in his office. He might have slept on the floor the night of the funeral, but he needed something else for the nights to come. We raided the linen closet for some sheets and tucked them in as best we could. We had to take a pillow out of Susie's room. Mom had not left any extras out.

I took one look at the small bed we put together for him.

"Dad, you should take my room. This room looks . . . it looks . . . well, it looks too small for you."

I must have looked pretty shocked because he answered right away.

"JK, I'll be fine in here. It's just the way it needs to be right now. Go on, go to bed. Get some sleep, kid."

He sort of grabbed my ear, and his big hand stayed on my shoulder a little while. It hurt to see him shuffle away to the cot. He was still staring at the pillow when I left the room.

I walked up the staircase of photographs again.

I took the steps two at a time.

"I thought about your question."

I approached the woman in the black hat. She was standing in that place where I saw her the first day. She was even in the same clothes. So was I, but that was my uniform, my protection. Her sharp black eyes took me in. It was the usual punk outfit for me, not as extreme as I used to wear. Still, it had to be foreign to this elegant lady. My nose ring might have put her off; I saw the corner of her mouth twitch when she looked at it.

"Yes."

That was all the invitation I would get for a conversation. "I *am* bitter. Why did you ask?"

It was her turn not to answer.

"So, who died?" she asked.

"My sister."

"How old was she?"

"Same as me."

Susie's image flicked through my View Master. A cute kid. Serious girl. My best friend. My savior. A doctor. A beautiful woman. A patient. A shadow. Gone.

I eked out, "We're the same."

The woman nodded as if some film of the past had rolled through her mind too. Maybe hers was a black-and-white movie reel. She was starting her play. I was along for the ride.

"It's hard for me to come here. But I keep doing it. Why is that?"

She looked at me straight on, her intent clear: be sure to give me a proper answer this time.

"It's the grave, I think. Susie, my sister, she calls me from in there." I answered as best as I could, given her challenging question.

"I don't think that's it, at least not in my case. Maybe the guilt." Francine said.

"Yeah, maybe."

I stood next to the lady in the black hat instead of being at Susie's grave. We didn't say anything else that day. She pretty much left me hanging there with the idea of guilt. I didn't realize it then, but she was a master and I a puppet. At least for a while.

She was right. It could be the guilt.

This lady might have a story like mine. No. Nothing could be as bad as mine.

Chapter 2

Splits—Then and Now

Susie never gave up on me. She couldn't. It was in her genetic code: Must save JK.

Mom didn't see things the same way; she thought it was all too out of balance. "Too extreme, Susie. It's too much for you." is what Mom shouted one of the many nights Susie came to my rescue while we were growing up.

Mom was undone by it all; Susie, not at all. Susie even tried to do something about my wardrobe. She was not a fan of the eighties punk outfits that I favored. I argued that black was timeless, but Susie disagreed.

I should thank her, though. She taught me to look at the world with some color. It helped with the Hollywood crowd that one season that we had. The producer never quite got how a kid like me could know about the designer shoes and handbags the actresses came in with before changing into their copycat costumes of what I wore.

I'd like to think it was my deep affection for Susie that glued me by her side at the end. But no. It was in my genetic code: Must witness Susie die.

The guilt and sadness came along as freeloaders. It surprised me just how much of a hole she left in my life. Not as deep as my own induced depression of a few years back, but more lasting. Everlasting.

Being incomplete gets complicated. We shared cells and water before we were born and during our whole lives. Then Susie vanished. Or did she? She was not quite gone: I was still here.

Mom started bringing flowers into the house, changing them every three or four days to ensure no fading or drooping. These were bright, gaudy flowers encroaching in our place of mourning—an exclamation mark in an otherwise contrite, constricted house. It was vexing, all this freshness.

For weeks we roamed, Mom, Dad, and I, crisscrossing the traces of each other. Nothing was real enough to hold us to our house or each other. The occasional conversation was limited to the essentials unless one of us had some gumption. Dad tried hard with me. I softened up some. My anger was jelly—I could cut it, but the chewing was a disappointment. This was no steak.

Dad stuck to his office and the cot. "To do some work," he said. What a retired man works on, I didn't ask. He was fragile, our Dad. My Dad that is.

He was such a prominent figure for Susie and me when we were kids. The engineer always explaining to us how things were put together. He thrived on sharing his knowledge with us. So proud of himself, so sure. Susie and I would sit with him and listen to his deep voice until—well, until that series of moments when we grew up, one inch at a time. As our lens on the world became bigger, we didn't see Dad anymore. He figured it out on the day we did not sit still for his explanation about the 1982 Columbia space shuttle crash. He soon stopped with the talk. He had no other way to communicate with us.

Dad without his daughter shrank back into himself. He couldn't stand it when things came apart, things with no wires and no instructions for his finely tuned mind. Things like his daughter's death.

His only words when Susie came to tell him she was dying were, "No, honey. That can't be right. No. No." She told me about that later, how he kept saying "No," as he crushed her into him, stroking her hair. Then he let her go and walked away. Just left.

He still had me, the other child. JK. He came out to the porch when he heard me tap on his door with the beer.

"Good day to you, JK."

"Yeah, to you too, Dad."

"Doing any writing?"

"Just some thinking."

"About a story?"

"Yeah, about a story."

"That's good."

He didn't know it was Susie's story running through my mind. He needed to hang on to something, something positive. I gave him gentleness through omission. We covered the same old ground in our conversations for a while . . . until I started to tell him about Francine.

Mom and Dad had never moved. They got lucky and bought before the housing bubble in one of the many towns around Stanford. "Well, it was just too good to be true," Mom used to say. They were stable, sedentary folks by nature. The house Susie and I grew up in stayed there for us to visit after we both went to college, me to Berkeley and Susie to Princeton followed by Stanford Medical School.

When Susie had her last stint at Stanford Medical Center, we were all home for her transformation from young doctor to patient. Before that, it had been blue-chip universities for us both. It goes to show just how much that Ivy education is worth.

This was like no other homecoming, but Susie and I had some traditions I decided to honor. The ice cream parlor was one of them. The Peninsula Fountain and Grill, a timeless example of Americana, was where Susie and I shared our banana splits while growing up. We never ordered anything else. She liked the strawberry ice cream and vanilla. I preferred chocolate and could be talked into vanilla. That is how we split things ever since we were little. We were lucky it was within walking distance of our house; Mom would let us go once a week on our own.

"There you go, honey." As old as the parlor, the redheaded waitress set down the famed split in front of me. The management recently renovated to red and green vinyl booths and chairs, but the face-lift couldn't get the memories out of my head.

"Thanks, Pearl."

"That's OK, honey. You go ahead now."

She put her hand on my shoulder and then tapped me forward as if she were a coach and I a promising athlete.

I held up my spoon. At the ready, I was waiting for the start signal. But memories beckoned. The split called me to one of our last splits.

"JK, I think you should start writing again," my little baldie of a sister insisted over the ice cream.

"Nah, Susie. It's just not there. Come on, let's eat our ice cream."

"JK, listen to me. This is important. It's your life!"

Her blue eyes were without eyelashes. They were piercing right into the heart of things.

"Susie, girl, now you stop it. We need to focus on you and getting you better."

"Your writing would help me get better." She grinned madly.

She waved her spoon around and licked her lips. She had almost finished her strawberry ice cream.

"What about that experimental treatment? The one where they zap your cells with light?"

"Too late for that."

"What do you mean too late? Susie, how could it be too late? You just got diagnosed!"

"JK, stop it."

"Stop what?"

I could play stupid with the best of them.

"Stop denying it. The only thing that can help is a bone marrow transplant."

"So, let's get you one."

But Susie knew. She was a doctor. She knew her best chance was with me. Genetics dictated there was one out of four chances that I could be a match.

But I wasn't much of a catch: two years out of rehab and more than that in years of abuse before then. No, I wasn't a catch, and neither were my cells.

"JK, you know what?"

"What, Sis?"

"Hey, you know chocolate isn't all that bad. I think I'll have some of yours. Do you mind?"

As if I could keep anything of mine from her at a time like this.

Susie already suspected what would soon be made clear to me. I was a bone marrow match for her—genetically, that is—but I couldn't donate. I had hurt my body too severely with drugs. I was not healthy enough, the doctor said. I swore something fierce at that white coat, but there was no budging him. The man denying me a savior's role for Susie said I was free to consult with other experts. He was confident that no one—emphasis, *no one*—would put a donor like me at risk with the harvesting procedure.

"What about Susie's risk?" I asked him.

No answer ever came. I was no use to Susie whatsoever. Just comic relief. Days on end in the various waiting rooms, I was with her . . . she still glamourous, and me, the recovering addict all torn up. I don't think the other patients knew which one of us was in to see the doctor unless Susie's wig revealed itself for the fake it was. The slow look of illumination on their faces would make for good TV.

Susie and I went back to the ice cream parlor one more time, but the old rules didn't apply anymore. She had a few spoons of everything on the split. So did I. She looked happy as she made her way through the ice cream.

"That's it, JK. A new world order for both of us."

She smiled. I could see a halo around her. Susie held onto me on the way out. She could barely walk on her own. But I was there. I was finally there with her, for her, just as she had been for me.

So, I sat at the ice cream parlor in front of this new split, wishing it was the old one. I watched it melt. The spoon was in my hand, at the ready. But I wasn't.

"JK, no worries. Maybe next time."

Pearl came over and blocked the view out to the street. I could see her roots showing signs of time; she could put things right with Clairol or some such. For me, there were no easy answers.

Pearl picked up the untouched plate and my spoon. She had laid out Susie's spoon when this whole mess started. It was cold. I took it with me when I left.

Francine was shivering in front of the same grave, still in the same outfit. Temperatures were variable this time of year, and today was chilly. The next time I came, I would bring her Susie's shawl.

"So, who's this?"

Francine looked at me from underneath her black hat. It framed her face just so.

"Oh, he was my husband, I suppose. After a fashion. We were married anyway."

My antenna shot up. And so it began.

"Were you married for a long time?"

"We knew each other when I was very young."

Not the most precise answer. I started to work. "So, high

school sweethearts?"

"School? No, no. Not school. The war." She laughed bitterly. "Not the usual education."

What war? How old was Francine? She noticed my confusion.

"Young people. What do you know? It was the Second World War. Cruel war, evil time."

She pursed her lips. I could see her wrinkles snapping to attention. "He was an officer. A good one. At least not so bad."

A huge sigh. Seriously, was she an actress? I couldn't tell.

"So, you were how old?"

"Just a girl. Yes, a little girl. Very spoiled. Young. I knew so little."

"Errr . . . so you were?"

"Very spoiled. Yes, very."

She stroked her chin. She was maddening.

"OK, then. I should head off . . . ."

"I was twelve. Twelve years old."

She admitted that as if under duress.

"Twelve? That seems awfully young to get married."

Was she deliberately obtuse with me?

A small giggle, girlish, came from the expertly made-up lady next to me. "No, no, we weren't married until years later. He managed to track me down. Narrowly escaped himself, I must say. It wasn't easy for the Germans at the end of the war, you know."

Germans? Wait. She was not German. I was sure of that much.

"I must go now. Someone is waiting for me."

She had baited me and didn't need to say anything else just then. She took a few steps and then turned back. "I'll see you next week then?"

"Yes, next week."

The carving on the headstone we had been standing at said:

Franz Giettester
Husband
1910 - 2004

Not much there.

I went over to Susie's grave. I had the spoon with me. I was going to plant it in the ground, but I saw Mom had brought flowers from the house. The spoon would just look stupid. I couldn't do that to Susie. She cared about looks.

"Susie, Susie, Susie," I called her.

No answer.

I sat down on the damp ground and started to warm up the spoon with my thumb. I could see my distorted face on the smooth surface of the spoon. Was I as warped as I looked? Tears. Finally. Spilling out. I watered the ground that day.

Mom wiped the grime off my face when I got home. One

look at me, and she turned around smartly, away from me, her wide skirt snapping around her slim figure. Like Susie, she also cared about looks. Standing in our foyer, I was sick at the thought of being alone. But Mom came back before I could start up again with the tears. She produced a warm wet towel and cleaned up her remaining daughter.

"JK. Oh. I know. I know, child. Hush. Hush now."

It was a whisper. It was an order.

She looked straight at me. My Mom could also be the nurturer, the consoler. I didn't always give her credit for the other pieces of herself. She was so close I could smell her perfume mixed in with the hairspray. I breathed it all in, the familiar smell.

"Mom? I . . . ."

I what? Had a spoon in my pocket? I met a woman in a black hat? I managed to cry? What could I lay claim to?

Mom did not hesitate; she did not want us to stay in the abyss. She led me away, back towards the more manageable world where she could provide some comfort.

"Come on. Let's get you back together, and we can see about dinner."

With a squeeze on the same shoulder Pearl had connected with at the ice cream shop, Mom walked past me into the kitchen. She didn't have to turn back. I followed her. There was a dinner to put together. The general needed a sous-chef, and I had just been enlisted.

It was the practical matters we all clung to without Susie.

One day into the next. And so it went. Dad in his office with his faithful cot. Mom was home only to make dinner; other than that, the flowers were the only sign of her presence in the house. That, and the wet towel one afternoon.

And me, in limbo, tethered only by a stranger in a black hat.

Chapter 3

Families

"Where is it, JK? Where did you put it?" Mom shook me awake. I managed to sit up among the mess of sheets of my bed.

"What?"

"Susie's shawl! Her shawl! What did you do with it?"

Ah, the shawl. I was going to give it to Francine. She had been cold at the cemetery. I had placed in my bag so I wouldn't forget it.

"Well, err . . . Mom, I lost it."

I didn't see the slap coming. Stung like hell. The warrior's slap to the oh-too-deserving heathen child. The only one left to slap. Mom was immediately horrified; her mouth was a perfect O shape.

I, on the other hand, couldn't work up enough energy to get mad at her. I had a date to keep. My feet hit the ground, and I untangled myself from the bed. I pushed my way past the confused combatant before we slipped into even more dangerous territory, and I became a bona fide enemy.

Francine beamed when I offered her the shawl.

"You are very kind. My, how thoughtful for a young person such as yourself."

She wasn't talking about my age, not really. She recovered quickly and smiled.

"Well, you seemed cold last week."

"This shawl is very fine."

"It belonged to my sister. She only bought quality clothes."

An uneasy silence hung about us. Francine kept the shawl on her arm. I realized she might not wear it now. I imagined Francine had a sense of decency. I would soon find out that was totally alien to her.

"I should introduce myself. I am Francine. You are?"

"JK."

"It stands for . . .?"

"JK. Just JK, thanks."

No need to elaborate.

"Alright, then; just JK."

She smiled again, looking much younger for a moment. And then she surprised me. She slipped her hand through my arm and started to walk through the cemetery, away from her husband and my sister. She walked steadily in her fragile shoes, me in tow with my stylized combat boots. Careful steps, as if the precise path we followed had a meaning.

"Look, look there. What a beautiful angel sculpture. And there, a male cardinal. Listen. Yes, that's it. Fall is glorious, don't you think? Those squirrels . . . where do they get the energy?"

It was a meditation walk. She spoke only of what we saw. The two of us crept around the decrepit cemetery, looking at tiny marvels poking out from every corner. It was soothing to be led around the dead by this stranger, in turn lulled by her voice and then squeezed to attention by her bony hands.

Francine was shorter than me. We made quite a pair walking in this un-American fashion. But then, what could be more American than the diversity of the two of us? We were not quite the melting pot, of course; but we would melt into each other's story for a while.

She didn't need to ask me as she left me at the gateway. I would be there the next day.

Fall was in full swing, with no trace of warmth left. The colors were fantastic. To me, the natural beauty was perverse. All that evidence of "the life cycle" felt like a sledgehammer through my emptiness.

These unspoken feelings of mine intersected the talk coming from Mom. She told Dad and me she was seeing a therapist. She called this person a bereavement counselor.

Something about a women's group too. Mom became chatty. The torrent of regurgitated expressions from the counselor was painful to me. The words became her mantra, spoken out loud over and over, heaped onto Dad and me. I tried to ignore it, but Mom didn't want to be ignored.

We were having dinners now, again. Three plates at the table. Our new number.

"So, JK. What are your plans? Must move forward, you know."

"Hmmm."

"I'm waiting, JK. We're all waiting."

"Seriously, Mom. I'm working on something."

"How exciting. Tell me more. Is it the same genre as before? I never understood it all. Susie tried to explain the genius of it all. She said that about you, you know. Genius."

"Genius?"

"Genius. That's what she said about it."

"Susie was always generous like that. No one else thought it was genius. I was just trying to make a buck."

Mom stared at me, her remaining child, trying hard to do it through Susie's eyes.

"Let JK be, Patrice. It's still too fresh."

The big clumsy guy remembered he was a father. Mine.

"No worries, Dad. No worries."

I learned that from a young British actress on my show. These unique expressions in her natural speech would disappear into inner-city American as soon as she was on the set.

Genius, I had said at the time—overused word.

"Mom, I can't say yet what it will be. But I promise to explain it to you when it's done, so you don't miss out."

I grabbed my plate and headed back out to the porch, not feeling generous on that particular day.

"Susie girl, hush. I am trying to be good. It's just a slip."

Even the flowers could not spruce us up without Susie. She had been the peacemaker at times like these. We no longer had her connective tissue in the house, so it was up to each of us to channel her spirit.

I sat in the rocking chair, the plate at my feet. No beer—it wasn't worth going back in through the gauntlet. I heard my parents' hushed voices, some dishes clanging about, a chair being pushed back, a door closed shut. Then nothing. The house was dead silent.

Outside, I rocked like mad in the chair. The creaks came fast and furious on the old deck's uneven floorboards. The upgrade of the deck was something Dad had not gotten around to. The chair and I rattled fiercely, the plate clanking along in moderation. The gaps between the deck's wood planks revealed themselves, happy to have a role in the scene. The wide wood beams fought the long nails meant to keep them all in place. Things usually start well put together until someone comes a' rocking. With my mad, careless, futile rocking, I was challenging the world order in my small universe.

I stopped.

Impotent.

All this space between us without Susie to fill it. Hell. Not much left.

The following day, I found Francine sitting at one of the solid benches in the cemetery. The sky was alarmingly gray. Rain could come at any time. As a small act of charity, the sun would not taunt me today. I could manage the gray; it was close enough to black.

Francine's hat was gone. I saw how sweet her face must have been. The red lipstick was still there, and her purse sat neatly on her lap. Both legs were straight, and her feet were on the ground, side by side, like two soldiers.

"Ah, you're here. Come sit."

And I did. Right next to her.

"I saw your sister's grave. At least, I believe it was hers. You're a little older than I thought."

"Older, but not wiser."

Still wisecracking. Still lame.

Francine was serious. "Wise enough. Pain does that. How did she die? An accident?"

"A chromosome accident. She must have grabbed the wrong batch."

"Ah, an illness," Francine nodded. "Was it long?"

"Long enough."

"And you were close? I mean . . . ."

"Yes, we were very close. She saved my life. I owe her every-thing. Everything."

The confession came out faster than I thought possible. Francine's followed.

"Me too. I owed my sister. Never did repay her."

"A sister! You have a sister?"

All of me was at attention. Another sister! The thought had never entered my mind.

"Pretty obtuse of you, JK," Susie was saying in my mind, probably rolling her eyes.

"Yes. Older by several years. Quite lovely in her way. She was . . . well, she was straight. You know?"

Francine looked directly into my eyes, keen to make sure I got her meaning.

I understood straight. It was not my nature, but it had been part of Susie's and highly annoying at times. No, that was unfair of me. Susie was straight, but she was wise, funny, loving, devoted, and all those words older women trot out when showering compliments to our generation. The truth was, Susie was great. Great in my world and in the wide world out there where all the other women live.

I shrugged off Francine's stare. The weight of the gray sky started to close in. I wanted to move that heaviness off me.

"How much older was your sister?" I asked.

"Oh, four years in age. Much older when it came to maturity, shall we say. It got her into trouble, all that sense of responsibility."

"How so?"

"Oh . . . ." and she waved her hand.

A tiny, well-manicured hand with red fingernails. An old hand. Much touching, no doubt.

Francine's story lay in the sister. I could smell it as certainly as the French perfume from Francine's delicate, wise, wrinkled wrist.

We were Jews. We didn't practice much, so we never got it right. At least that was my private personal joke. For Christmas, we had a tree and presents. The other Jews, the better ones, didn't have that. At least not the tree. I can't be sure about the gifts.

We went to see "Schindler's List." It was requisite viewing for all us Jews. Mom said so. Susie and I were in college at the time, but still impressionable kids. Susie grabbed my hand during the worst of it. Her beautiful face was rapt with disgust and disbelief. For me, I marveled at the monumental task of telling the story with the kind of images that would stick to your memory.

"JK, that was unbelievable. Horrible. So many people just gone because of one man. He spawned all that evil."

"Yep. Great movie."

My mind was processing the expanse of it all, the music, the dialogue, the visuals. I wondered: How did something like that film come together?

"Is that all you're going to say? Really?"

Susie was bewildered. Not her usual state. I wanted to abandon my analysis to meet her where the emotions were the topic, but I missed.

"He was awful, alright."

"I don't believe you, JK! All those people dead, and that's the best you can come up with?"

I had come up short. My sister turned away, got hold of Mom and Dad, walked with them, her long blonde hair breezily waving at me as I paddled behind them, trying to get back to our zone. I should have paid more attention to Susie, but I was absorbed by what would become my lifelong distraction: stories and the task of telling them. I started writing in earnest at that moment. Yet, at the very same time, I gave up a part of my sister.

At home that night, Mom tried to start a conversation as she set the table for dinner.

"So, what did you girls think of the movie?"

Neither one of us answered. The rift was ours, not to be shared with our parents. Silently we sat down for dinner.

Even Dad tried to get us back to safer ground. "Interesting, it was in black and white. Don't you think?"

"There was a spot of red, Dad."

The little girl's red coat had struck me. I would later hear about it in all the reviews. Maybe I was precocious. Or perhaps I was just like all the rest of them.

"Red, black, and white. Who cares?!" Susie boiled over.

"Susie, honey, what's wrong?"

Mom reached out to her daughter.

"I don't want to talk about it. It was a horrible movie!"

And for the second time, Susie turned away, this time from all of us. She left the table, which was unheard of in our approximate Jewish household. My parents exchanged a long look.

Mom and Dad always encouraged us to think. Well, Susie was thinking alright. I went up to her room that night and sat with her on the narrow bed.

"JK?"

"Yeah, Sis, I'm here."

"You know what bothers me?"

"What?"

"Hitler was only one man, a really evil man. So why did the ordinary people of Germany follow him? I mean, why didn't they see what he was doing and stop it?"

"Dunno. Herd mentality, I suppose."

"I'm scared."

"Susie, nothing like that will ever happen again."

"It's not that, JK. I'm scared I might not stand up for what's right."

I looked at my sister, sitting in her jammies in her tiny bed, girlhood remnants on display all around. She was going to be one hell of a woman.

"Sis, you have to believe me. You are not anything like those people."

I don't think I spoke more honestly in my life.

"How do we know until we're tested?"

"Look at you now. That's how you know."

I left her there, taking in my words. I left her so she would not see the doubts I had about my less-solid self. It was the first time I was aware of the uncertainty that inhabited me. It would come gushing out soon enough for all to see.

We would travel separate roads from then on, me flailing some, then flailing much. She was steadfast always. Almost always.

We crossed into each other's lives over and over again. Usually for banal exchanges, the kind that cements what was started in the womb, the sharing of nutrients to make us whole.

She saved my life.

I was with her when she died.

Those were the most prominent intersections of our lives. Our parents were extraneous to our being. Or so we made it appear. We were unfair to them.

I was on my own now. Susie was fading, her image slipping in my rearview mirror. Funny. She usually did things well. It must be me making a mess of it.

Francine was wrapped in Susie's shawl, sitting by herself or, rather, with herself. I held two Dunkin' coffee drinks. I handed one over to her. The cemetery was quiet, calm.

"Your sister?" I asked.

Impatience led to unnecessary roughness; the ref would have thrown a red flag on that play. The night had not been good to me. At least the sun was less insulting. The offense of the day had shifted to the night.

Francine chose silence in response. I simmered there on the bench next to the French woman wrapped in my sister's cashmere shawl. I remember asking my colorful sister why she chose black.

Susie had said, "Just coming around to your point of view, JK." She still had all her hair but had been losing some of her strength. Treatments were just starting.

"Since when do you take any fashion cues from me?"

I would not let her give up her colors so easily.

"It's just as you said. Black is timeless. I do listen to you. You know that."

She pinched me. Her mischievous smile came right after. I let it go at that—a small win in the JK column.

Back in the cemetery, Francine finally spoke. "Judith was my sister's name."

"Judith. Is that a Jewish name?"

Francine would not answer this question, but she talked about Judith and her family. At last, she opened windows to her past.

"Our family was well off. My father had a successful law practice. People went to him for all sorts of things. He was highly respected. Judith and I were always proud to go out with him, the silly girls that we were. Vain. Proud."

Francine paused and collected herself.

"Judith had started to think about her career and what she would do, you know, later on. 'A doctor,' she said. Our father was so happy. Mom was a little worried; she wondered if that would leave time enough for a husband and a family."

She stopped. This time the past needed a moment before she picked up again.

"My father died early in the war, defending our country. The French are not, as a rule, brave or organized. Imagine sending a man accustomed to writing letters and documents to fight. He had never held a gun in his life! Ah, the French were stupid at that time and cowardly. Just a few men and women had courage. Of course, the women suffered more. My father must have been brave, though."

"You don't know?"

"No. We were cut off very quickly from any communication. France was occupied rather early. We were among the first to welcome German troops."

There was a slight tremble in her voice when she said the word "welcome." I pushed back the surge of images; Francine's words would bring their own. Slow down, JK.

"He was very striking, you know. Tall like our father. Not handsome. No, not handsome at all. Male. Strong. Good at taking. Took it all in the end."

"Who?"

"The captain who set up in our house. We had a wonderful property, so sophisticated. It was my mother's pride—well, after her family, of course. It turned out to be suitable for a German officer of his standing. Ironic, don't you think? All her hard work, only to get such a—well, such a prize, I suppose."

"Oh, I can imagine."

Something was punching out through the years. It was a tragedy, a real-life drama, as a publicist would say.

Francine nodded, wise to the ways of the world.

"Maybe you can imagine JK. Or maybe you can't. You see, my mother tried to make our home uninhabitable. She ruined our pipes, hoping it would discourage the Germans. That only made us all have to use the outside privy. Very inconvenient, especially for young girls. She miscalculated. The Germans would not give an inch. Admirable in a way, but her efforts were futile in the end."

Francine pursed her lips again. I could not make out the real sentiment towards her mother. Could it be disdain?

I tried to get more information.

"Your mother sounds like quite the lady."

"Does she? I've forgotten. She had trouble with even the simplest things after the captain moved in. She lost herself when Papa left. My sister and I were a terrible reminder of him, not to mention of her responsibilities. She gave up on that last piece."

I had to get back to the basics.

"Your mom . . . what happened to her?"

"What happens to women who give up? Someone came along to finish her."

"She was killed?"

"Killed? Yes, I suppose she was. Yes, she was killed."

Francine was hiding something—many somethings. I made a note to come back to it all, then scrapped it. She had to lead.

"And you? And your sister?" I asked.

"Us? Well, Judith ended up having to see to the Germans, after my mother."

No mention of what happened to her mother or to her sister exactly. I thought back to what I knew of that time. History mixed up with social reinterpretation and movie images on top of it all.

The Dunkin' cup in my hand had gone cold. By the time I got back with a warmer cup, Francine was gone. I went to see Susie for a silent visit. Not much to tell her yet.

At home, Dad was in his office. I listened at the door to the clicking of his hands on the keyboard, sounds of productivity which made me smile. My turn may yet come. Mom rushed in from the outside, flowers in hand to replace the ones from last week.

"JK. Come give me a hand."

I passed by the small refuge of Dad's office. He called out to me.

"In a bit, Dad." It was Mom's turn.

I got to my mother's kitchen a few moments later. She cleared her work surface. It was going to be her and the flowers. She reached up to the upper shelves and brought down all her vases to find the right one. In the end, she selected a basic florist vase rather than the cut crystal she often favored.

"They say doing your usual activities can be a good thing."

She held a sharp knife, which moved along the stems, her hands willing to do the damage needed for a longer life in the vase. As if the flowers' longer life mattered.

"Who's that, Mom?"

"The women in the group. The women in my bereavement group. Really, JK, I told you about them a few weeks ago now."

"So, these women. Who are they exactly?"

"Just women. They've all been through something like this. A daughter or son. Or their husband, I guess. Yes, that's right; for one of them, it's a husband."

Mom went on to describe their grief in snippets. I wasn't sure about this conversation or the group, so I focused instead on the flowers getting pruned. The hacking continued. Each time, I winced. Mom's hands were certain for a while. Life had to be extended. Then she started again with the talking.

"Usual activities. The more, the better, I figure. Stops the pain."

Mom put down the knife. She was on a break from doing violence to the flowers. After a long pause, she moved towards me in a flash.

"What do you think, JK?"

No more hiding. She came right at me.

"Well, Mom, I guess they know what works for them."

I hoped she would fill in the rest for herself.

"What are you saying, JK?"

Nope, straight back onto me again. No luck. I wanted to walk away, but the knife held me still, a hostage in the scene. If this had been on television, a well-weathered cop would negotiate for my release. Dad was perfect casting for the role. But he was in his office, and I had moved past him. I was on my own.

I dove in.

"Mom, don't you think we each react in our way? I don't see how these strangers can have answers for you. What do they know about you? About Susie?"

"That's right, JK. Only you and your father know about Susie. And neither one of you talks to me. You're not, you're not . . . available."

There. No more blanks to fill. It was my fault. And Dad's too. Mom poured out her heart to strangers because of us. Huh. Of course, *I* was deficient. But Dad, too? I had never considered that.

"That's not fair."

"It's how I feel, JK. Fair, not fair. Who cares? Who cares?"

The knife may have been set down, but the daggers still came at me.

I walked away then before it got any worse. Susie wasn't there to help smooth over my roughness. I had to cope on my own.

Dad's office door was still open. I didn't look in.

Up the stairs. With the pictures for company. And my thoughts. Mom might have a point there. None of us were any good at communicating.

Who cares anyway? Mom had the right question. Pinpoint accuracy on that one.

Chapter 4

Days Move—We Don't

Days hung around us, dreary until they moved into night. I was out with Dad on the porch not long after the knife-and-flower incident. Mom and I steered clear of each other, but her words rang on and on in my head.

The stars were out. The neighbors no longer treated us like a variety show. Dad had been there a while, just staring out at the sky. He used to show us the constellations. The only one I could still find reliably was the Big Dipper and sometimes Andromeda. The rest faded into the tapestry of shininess, romance, deception, blackness.

"I miss her, JK. I miss Susie."

Desolation itself looked up at me from my father's eyes.

I sat down in the chair next to him to equalize things the best I could.

"Yeah, Dad. Me too."

It was six weeks or so since we buried Susie, but we kept some extended version of time with us.

"It's hard. You know?"

I knew.

"I talk to her. I talk to Susie all day long."

"Really? So do I. I go to the cemetery."

"Not the same, though, is it?"

"No, not the same."

Susie would want me to try and connect. I decided I should.

"You know, Mom says we're not talking to her. She's upset about it."

"I can see her point of view."

"So?"

"So what, JK? So what?"

"Should we?"

"Should we talk? Kid, that's what we're doing. Right?"

He patted me on the knee. His eyes wandered off, away from what I was saying to him. Dad was slipping away from our haven on the porch. Funny, he had never been slippery before. Solid, Susie always said.

The squeak of the porch door announced my mother.

"Roger? Give us a moment, would you?"

"Sure, Patrice. JK, you can talk to me anytime, kid. Anytime."

He crushed my shoulder. It hurt some; love does sometimes.

Mom sat down on the edge of Dad's seat, not entirely committed to the chair. Maybe she couldn't stand even that degree of overlap with her husband, or perhaps she wasn't quite sure how long she'd stay. The warrior was silent a long time; she was waging some great battle. Later, I realized her struggle was for me. Mom was trying to commit to me.

"JK, I . . . I want to us to talk. Can we do that?"

My turn to be silent. I was not ready for this. Not yet.

"Honey? Can we at least try?"

What did she think I was doing? This was my best impersonation of trying. I might even get there, get to where she was—someday.

"OK. OK then, JK."

Another squeak of the porch door announced we would both have to try again.

"These things take time." Who said that? Someone was talking. Somewhere, words were spoken.

My nerves were oddly smoothed out the next day. My mind was in such overload that nothing but calm could rise to the surface, or I would be engulfed. Somehow, I had managed an airtight box around it all.

The cemetery was busier than usual. Other families were burying their loved ones that Saturday. I saw a small girl standing with her mother. Beside them a father, a husband, even. He had his arms wrapped tight around his wife, who held the girl close to her. They were united for a time, strong and solid. When they walked away, only the little girl seemed to know her place. She ran after one of the squirrels, delighted to stretch her legs. Her tiny lungs filled the air with a happy laugh.

Her mom called out to her. "Cindy! Cindy! Come on now. I told you this is not a park. No running. Show some respect."

"Let her go, Nancy. Let her be." The father came over to his wife. "She needs to run. She's just a kid."

"Still, Nate, your mother wouldn't approve."

"Oh, darling. We must focus on the living. Right?"

"Nate, of course. Of course, you're right." And then to her daughter, she said, "Cindy, don't be too long now. We have to head home soon. Maybe we'll stop for ice cream, sweetheart."

Dead stop from the little legs. "Ice cream?" More laughter. Back to her parents, the little one ran.

"Let's go." The man led his two women away from the sadness. His job was done for the day. He would start again soon, no doubt. A man had to earn his spot at regular intervals.

Was I watching a script? Sure, I was. It was easier to manage a script.

"Focus on the living. Hmmm. Yes, I like that." Francine said.

She was watching the little girl, too, her eyes drawn to the same scene. She stood close to me while the family disappeared into the distance. She wore a different tailored suit; this one was brown. Also a classic, but I could not pin a label on it. It was a thick tweed, better to handle the weather as we moved into winter. Maybe she would even wear a coat soon. I certainly had taken to my leather jacket.

"Banal. Terribly banal," I said.

It was a technical assessment.

"My dear JK. Universal truths are uninspired at best. That is why it is so easy to miss them. I do agree with that man, however. It is the living we must focus on."

I was talking about the script while Francine was back in the real world.

"Come. Perhaps today we should leave this place. A café, perhaps? I know a place. It's a bit of a walk, but we should take our cue from the little one and get some exercise."

"Hmmm."

"Come now, JK. Let's go."

And with that, she winked at me. Or her eyelid twitched. Some script.

I was surprised by her brisk pace. Those little heels looked too delicate to support her athletic speed. I was not in any great shape; we arrived with the younger one of us winded. She must have been a dancer. I only ever worked my fingertips on the keyboard. It was hard to keep up with Francine.

As a testament to the worldwide connectivity that binds us, Francine stopped at a French café in our fine American city. She ordered an allongé and a croissant beurre. The waitress had her repeat her order several times; Francine's proper pronunciation was not the norm for the clientele. I finally had to jump in with the American version of the words. "Ah, got it, thanks." Gratitude and relief from the waitress.

Francine was oblivious to the awkwardness, announced it was too early for pain au chocolat and handed the waitress her small menu.

"Same for me."

No need to overdo it.

"Back in a flash, ladies."

The girl's big toothy grin betrayed the fakeness of the café just then as if the dance with the order did not do enough of that. Francine's eyebrows shot up.

"Well. Look at that," she said, doubtless thinking no garçon in a French café would smile that broadly.

I held tight for the next wave.

"Children do have quite a bit of power, don't you think, JK?"

"Dunno. Never really thought about it."

"Oh, come now. Didn't you and your sister take over your parents' lives?"

"We were just us."

It had always been Susie and me first. Our parents were second. My reasons for sticking around now were murky. Mom and Dad were determined to reach me through the blur. Why? Family, love, Susie, desperation, grief, hope, habit. The list was long and inconclusive.

"I see. Well, perhaps there's something there to reconsider."

Francine was brilliant. Brilliant. Yes, something to reconsider. It had already started.

The waitress returned with the coffees. What do you know; it had been a flash.

"I'll be honest with you, JK. I was a selfish child. Terribly selfish. I think all children are."

A sigh. A small sip of the caffeinated sludge followed. Pursed red lips about to unfurl some other godless truth. And I sat there, out of time, out of place, hanging on every word. Susie and I had been selfish too. Too true.

"As the youngest, my parents and Judith humored me. As I grew up, I played for them, you know, acting the part to keep it all coming. They indulged me. I'm sure my parents had their faults, but they were good people. Very generous. So, I was the golden child. I think I mentioned I was spoiled."

Was that an actual twinkle of nostalgia in her eye? She must have had some childhood.

"I didn't understand when the war came why they should stop humoring me. Why should my world be any different? They did their best, especially Papa, before he left to fight. He did not want me to be afraid. Poor man. My mother too, for as long as . . . well, as long as she could."

Twinkle gone. Loss. More sludge.

"And then, then, my sister Judith. Despite the Germans in the house, I just wanted it all to continue."

Francine paused, the present taking over.

"Ah, the croissants are here."

As she ate, the flakes fell on the café table. One small hand swept them away into the other hand just at the table's edge, and then a tiny rub of both hands returned the flakes to the plate of origin. This was a well-practiced motion of returning that which had been used to its source in a reduced form. Hollywood did that to me. Returned me to Susie in pitiful shape.

Francine finished eating and picked up the thread. "Do you see, dear?"

"Sorry. See what?"

"How terrible I was."

"You haven't told me much."

"I've told you everything! You're listening, aren't you? JK, you're with me, aren't you?"

I was there alright. The images of all the little girls were right there with me. I had to get a fix on Francine, little Francine, before she came to sit with me. The story. I wanted that story, didn't I?

"JK, you're still very young."

"Nope, not anymore."

"But you are dear; you are. So much to learn."

Young? No, not so much. Not without Susie. And even with her, we both grew up. Up and away.

"Anything else, ladies?"

The toothy one was back to try and free up the table.

"The check, please."

Time to get away. I paid for the drinks and the croissants and stood while Francine remained sitting, looking at the neighborhood going about its day. I pitied the waitress if she tried to hustle this French lady along before she was ready to go.

"Goodbye, JK. Thank you for the treat. It was lovely. I enjoyed it so very much."

I wrapped my croissant in a napkin and took it with me. I munched on it as I walked home. My conversation with Francine was on a loop in my mind.

I flicked off the flakes before going into my parent's house. My black T-shirt was no longer speckled when I sat down at the table with my folks. The tenderness I reserved all my life for Susie spilled over to them that night over dinner. Mom won a concession from me; I would go into her world some the next day. Dad seemed relieved there was some motion, some emotion, other than distance.

There was not enough for our new number. Not yet.

Chapter 5

The Women

The bereavement group met near but not too close to the hospital. Too many memories, Mom explained. I followed Mom through the lobby as she headed to a back corridor. The room had a neutered corporate décor to match the primary office building. This was not where the colorful living of the city happened.

The women gathered in a circle—all sorts of women. I sat back in the corner; their territory was impenetrable, intimate, not for the likes of me.

Until then, I only spoke with Susie of the important matters. Not always the easiest of conversations, but always honest. At times brutal, with a loving wrapper at either end.

Like the time Susie came into my apartment and brandished one of the bottles right off the kitchen counter.

"JK, what the hell is all this?" She was angry. "Do you even know what you're doing anymore? This has to stop!"

Hands on hips, like a caped crusader with a bottle of cheap tequila, Susie would not let go.

"Suze, just let it be. OK?"

The woosh of the previous night made it hard to speak or stand.

"No. That isn't going to happen."

Susie's grip on the tequila was firm, just like her spirit.

"Come on. Give it back."

I made a swipe for it, but I landed on the floor instead. From that position, I took in the scene as Susie walked the bottle over to the sink. I watched my sister in her designer suit with a fancy scarf pour it out. The red silk kept falling off her shoulder. Susie put it back time and time again rather than taking it off. She was not the type to abandon something she loved.

"Susie, come on," I groaned.

"This is for your own good. Get up, JK. Get up off the floor. It's dirty."

I started to laugh, a light chuckle, which morphed into a laugh—more bottles at the sink. The mood dial went up a notch in the apartment. The red scarf got wet with the booze. That was not good. It did not help either that my one-night stand came out of the bathroom just then.

"Dude, is the party over? Whoa. Who is this? Hot!"

He threw in the lewd leer at my sister for free—gobble gobble. The scene was better than anything I could have written.

"Get out of here!"

Susie just shoved the hapless kid out. Half-naked. But in LA, who's to know that?

"JK, you have to pull yourself together." In a rage, she cleaned me out of all the booze. She even tied the wet scarf back out of the way for The Great Cleansing of JK. It would be a pain to replace all that booze; but I did not share that with my sister just then. It was a one-way conversation for a bit. She above, me below. The dirty floor suited me fine.

Susie finally crouched down to address the petulant child I had become.

"You don't answer the phone. You don't show up for our usual date. And you are out there screwing these losers and screwing up your life. You're better than this, JK."

"Nope, Susie, I don't think so. Not better. Look at me for what I am. Washed up. Come on Suze. Take a hard look."

I held her hands and pulled her up close. She did look. What she saw had nothing to do with me, and what she did even less so. Her bear of a hug enveloped my sweaty, slimy self on the dirty floor.

She rose after that.

"You listen to me, JK. I know you. I *know* you."

We repeated this scene for the better part of a year. Oh, there were some variations as time moved us forward on the sorry path. Drugs replaced booze. Or I added the drugs on top of the booze. My lovers were men or, sometimes, women. Some came in pairs. The wheel went round and round, with all sorts of little feet on it. Stinky feet.

I ended up on the streets when the money ran out. A kid from Palo Alto sunk into the crud of LA. It got worse then.

Only Susie knew. It was a blur to me. It still is. I wiped an entire year from my life, along with every other decent person I knew at the time, except for my sister. She was un-runnable. She always found me and cleaned me up.

Susie brought me to her place each time, and I broke her heart every single time. I was hungry for the pain. There was nothing ahead of me. She wasn't enough. That hurt us both, and it cemented us together. I could never shake her, no matter what I did. No matter how many lewd, crazy, evil, mean things I did and forgot. Susie erased them and forgave me.

I remember waking up in the hospital. She was standing over me in her white medical coat. Worried. Dark circles under those baby blues. She was stunning, my sister. Even then. Even later.

"JK? JK, can you hear me?"

"What happened?"

"You were beaten up. Pretty bad. You'll have some ugly scars. You're in the hospital."

"What? Where?"

"Doesn't matter, JK. The only thing that matters is that we're going to get you better."

And she took over. Rehab, the whole nine yards. I don't think she ever told Mom and Dad much. The rehab I remember almost too well. Sobering is a bitch, boys and girls. The payoff after that hell of a ride: well, not much better. There were a dull couple of years of odd jobs back in the "real world."

Then Susie showed up and told me it would get bad for her. Real bad.

The women in Mom's circle were nothing like Susie. Or they were everything she was. I didn't want to know. I didn't listen. I never heard their words, their beautiful, raw, gut-wrenching words. I made them up in my head. Each woman was a story; that's all that remained—a story.

"I still see him in his room," the woman at the meeting said. "He had a teddy bear, Alfie. He called him Alshie. You see, he had a little trouble with his speech. It was getting better, though. The speech therapist gave him the best exercises. He liked her so much, Miss Thurman. He was so serious for a five-year-old; she said it was a clear sign of intelligence. His sessions were forty-five minutes every Monday at four in the afternoon. These days, I just sit in the car outside her office. I am always on time now. He would have been seven last week. And cured, I'm sure. A play—he would have starred in a play by now. But, of course, he would have gotten a great role. Don't you think?"

Another woman said, "The only thing that keeps me going is knowing I will be with her someday. Or maybe I won't be good enough for that. Where is she anyway? It's so cold in the chapel when I go to pray. I don't think God is really there. Father Michael is a good priest, but he isn't a mother. A mother knows. 'There is no worse pain,' he says. Pain? I don't think this is pain. It's nothing at all. Nothing."

Another commented, "She was beautiful, you know. And talented. Everything a mother could hope for. Now? I just do the little I can manage. Some cooking, some cleaning. The laundry, of course. I don't want to go back to work. My memory is shot. I can't think straight. I can't read. I don't hear what people say to me. Does it get any better?"

And another said, "I broke down yesterday, right there in the Walmart. I couldn't remember the sound of his laugh, the sound of my little man's laugh. I was hysterical. The manager had to call my husband. I laughed and laughed. Imagine that. Steve said he was getting fed up with the calls. I kept laughing."

The women never responded to each other's stories. I saw no kindly looks or nods, no silent tears. I heard no words of support, no gasps. Each woman was perfectly alone in the circle.

I left. Mom knew I had been there. That was all there was. Two steps back.

My thumb could still get me a ride. I ended up in a bar that afternoon. The bottle of tequila right in front of me, my version of the women's words for company, and a few guys thrown in for yuks. I sent the guys away right quick. Some I had to talk to; my usual stare didn't quite deter them. The bottle shone in the gritty bar light, savior or oncoming train?

The women's stories whirled around until I got dizzy, time for the Dunkin' bagels.

"What do I owe you?" I asked the bartender.

"What? For sitting and staring at an unopened bottle of tequila? Nothing."

"OK, thanks."

"Come back if you like. The other customers talk too much."

With a wink, the beefy bartender turned away.

Nice ass. Who would have expected a spark in a dive like that?

"I'm JK, by the way."

The ass disappeared from my view and a well-chiseled chest turned back at me. "JK? Cool. I'm Patrick." Damn. And soft brown eyes. Lips, full. Argh, a mouth like that must be a gift from his mother's genes. Men with women's lips can get confusing. Trouble. It might even be the good kind. Something to tell Susie about. Maybe.

Susie and I had stopped that kind of talk a while back.

"Boys. Ugh."

Susie and I were late bloomers. Fourteen when she had her first kiss. Me, even later, with an acne-face guy who turned out to be a loser.

"So, blue eyes. Tell me."

Giggles. We still giggled back then.

Susie's cheeks were pink, and she was puffing. I had a feeling it was more than just that run up the stairs coloring my sister.

"Nah, nothing to talk about."

"What!? Are you going to keep me hanging, Sis? Not fair!"

"Well. It's private."

"Private? You're kidding, right?"

Took her a while, but she shared, coyly, incompletely, and breathlessly, with youth's hesitation and delight.

I turned out to be the adventurous one. I didn't share much either. I guess we were prudes around each other, or just plain careful not to overshare. It wasn't that kind of love with Susie.

It was better.

The women, the bar, Patrick. All behind me. The stories, though, I couldn't shake. They caught up to me as I rocked slowly on my parents' porch, madness replaced by contemplation.

Mom was on a bent knee.

"JK, honey. I'm sorry about all this."

I held onto my beer bottle; the water condensation replaced my absent tears.

"Hey, Mom. I'm sorry too."

"You know, your sister, she always had a way about her. Sweet on the outside but determined. You know that better than most."

Mom gave me a small smile.

Was the warrior exhibiting some humor? This had become a very curious house.

Mom continued, "People got confused about her. But Susie, she was always certain. That girl knew what she wanted right from the beginning. And you, JK, you were always what she wanted. First, when you were small, she wanted to play. Then she wanted to share all your adventures. Yes, yes, we knew about the dope in your senior year."

Gulp. They knew? Crap. I was in a mini tailspin, whereas Susie would have laughed it off with "Come on, JK, who cares after all this time!"

"OK, Susie. OK, I'm getting past it."

Geez, still pushy, that one.

"But you see, we thought it was great. It was perfect. You two kids would have each other for your whole lives. I messed that up. Your dad, he wanted another baby. But I just, I couldn't."

"Yeah, I know, Mom. You told us way back, remember? You made us promise to go in threes for our own families."

"I must have had an inkling clue. Mothers do."

"I guess."

"JK, you know she wanted to fight this thing as long as it made sense to. She was fearless, our Susie. Me, not so much right now."

Mom wiped at her eyes.

Tears? Tears again from the warrior? Mine were tucked away for the duration. Thank goodness I could still do a memory recall of dialogue.

"Mom? Are you alright?"

"Oh, honey!"

And my mother tried to take me back into her womb. We rocked. Not the mad rocking. The sweet, sad one.

Chapter 6

Legs Appear

"A skirt!? Josephine Kelly. What!?" Mom was apoplectic. She sat down, clutching her breast. "What is going on?" she demanded.

After all those years of carefully ignoring my genderless appearance, all the unasked questions came out in the most typical fashion. What *was* going on? All that pretense of being a good, understanding mother with no judgment and allowing herself no expectation was replaced by relief. Deep, breathe-again relief, the kind you can't hide.

Dad came out to see.

"JK, are you alright?" Total shock. Nothing else on my dad's face. No judgment, no relief. Well, maybe some genuine concern.

"Yep, sure am."

Both my parents were stunned by the sight of their

daughter's legs. I didn't have dress shoes, so I was in my Converse sneakers. But still, the legs were there. So were Mom and Dad, they stood closer to each other than they had since the funeral. As if staring at a version of their reborn daughter in the kitchen transported them back to the afternoon we buried Susie. Though maybe they were going farther back.

The skirt was loose; one of Susie's, of course. I had some breathing room from this womanly symbol, the symbol that tied me to the women in my mother's bereavement group. I had been going over their stories all night. Spinning, weaving them into a digest for a TV audience. I had a goal now.

"JK, what do we call you now?"

How do you answer a question like that from your father? You don't. It is impossible for a daughter to think her father wouldn't know what to call her. How far away was he from me? Time to get out, give them both a chance to recover. They would have something to discuss now.

"So. Any coffee? I have to get going. A meeting."

I punched Dad slightly in the arm with a sly grin before heading out to the cemetery.

Francine was more poised at my changed appearance. Although, in fairness, she didn't care about me, at least not like my folks.

"What a lovely young lady you are. Underneath all of that, I mean."

The last time I heard those words were on prom night from my dad. He beamed when I came down the stairs.

"What a lovely young woman you are, Josephine."

Susie was already in the living room with her prom date. She hugged me.

"Josie, that's super. Just like in the store when we picked it out. I'm so happy!"

She bobbed up and down. Her joy transferred over to me, and I started grinning until my mouth hurt.

Mom clicked a few photographs to show her friends her two beautiful daughters. My hair was long and brown. I had a touch of eyeliner and some colored lip balm. Susie had gone with Mom to the stylist; her whole face was made-up. But curiously, it looked even more like her.

"We'll wait with you until Freddie comes."

Only fair, I thought since I had waited a long time for him to ask me to the prom in the first place. He was not the school's best prize of a guy, but I liked him well enough. His acne scars might heal, and he had excellent hands. Soft. I had let him get under my blouse.

"Nah, Susie. You and Ron head off. We'll catch up."

"Are you sure?"

My sister was torn. Ron wanted to get out. Susie was his prize. I couldn't blame him.

"Sure. I'll see you there."

Ron didn't say much as he whisked her out the door. Smart enough to know he had to get out while the getting was still good. Ron's good fortune would not last long. Susie dumped him when she found out he knew all along about Freddie.

Mom and Dad waited with me. A rehearsal for what we were doing now without Susie. Back then, I still had a chance to be a good daughter, just like she was. And, of course, she was just out with a date then. Not in a box buried in the ground.

A while went by. Too much time passed for anything good to come of it. Mom and Dad exchanged worried looks.

"Let's redo your make-up, dear."

"Mom. No. Leave it alone."

"Some tea then?"

"Tea? No, Mom. That's for old ladies." I snapped at her.

"Josephine. Your Mom is just trying to help." Dad spoke firmly.

"You know Roger, instead of talking, hand me that phone. I am going to call that young man and . . . ."

"Mom!"

"Patrice!"

Dad had his arm around me, and we came apart with the force of our shrieks.

"Oh, never mind; I'll get it myself. You two would just wait here all night."

And my imperious mother walked over to the phone, dialed 411, got a number. I did not budge. Dad stayed with me. Glued back together, nothing like the tropical storm about to be unleashed by the woman on our kitchen phone.

"Mrs. Dunnett? Freddie's mom? This is Josephine Sandberg's mother, Patrice Sandberg. I'm calling . . . well, I am calling because we've been waiting for your son. It's the junior prom tonight, you know. Oh, I see. Hmmm. Indeed. A mix-up, you say? What? Do you think Josephine misunderstood? My daughter is a very clear-headed young lady, I'll have you know. No, she did not *imagine* a date! What kind of young man are you raising? I never! Well, I guess that's that then."

She hung up the phone and turned to Dad and me with the most inscrutable look. "Josephine, it appears this Freddie went to the prom with another young lady. That dim-witted mother of his was useless when I spoke with her."

"I am so sorry, Josephine."

Dad was badly beaten up; his shirt was getting soppy with my snot and my tears.

My mother was resolute. "Josephine Kelly, you pull yourself together. He is nothing, this boy. You and your sister are the most wonderful girls. You have a bright, bright future with boys much better than he is. Or without any boys. It's your choice, darling. Anything you want."

She was fierce, my Mom. I wanted to believe her, but I knew it wasn't so. I would be dumped over and over again.

We had cardboard pizza that prom night at home—the three of us. The fake jolliness resonated until it nearly became real laughter. Mom and Dad held hands going up the stairs. Mom tucked me in, just like old times. A kiss goodnight from her; it was almost OK.

Susie came home late, right into my room.

"What happened? Ron and I waited for you guys. Then Freddie showed up with that Susanna. JK, what's going on?"

I never answered.

She slept with me that night. She was wrapped up snugly right behind me, spooning me. Cradled by my sister still wearing her princess prom dress. Now she is cold and cracked. Something is not right when your memory is that good. Susie told me it was because of the writer in me.

"Sure, Sis. Sure."

"JK, are you here, dear?"

Francine gripped my forearm and called me back from the time warp, snapped away from the cuddles and the cracks. She gave me a few moments to recover before she continued.

"May I inquire what brought about this remarkable transformation?"

"Just a whim. This was my sister's skirt."

"Well, it is lovely, and so are you."

"Thank you."

Francine stared hard at my legs. My shoes must have thrown her off. Converse sneakers were not feminine to a woman like her.

It turned out that Francine was nervous.

"I need a favor."

"Sure. What do you need?"

"Actually, JK, it's . . . well . . . ."

"Yes? What?"

"I need a ride."

"A ride? A ride, that's it?"

"Well, it's enough, don't you think?"

"Where are we going?"

"Away. We're going away."

It was late, but the spark from the bar called me, and I was itchy. Francine and I would head off early the next day. She had only told me she needed to see someone.

I went to Patrick late on a Tuesday.

"Hey! JK, right?"

He was genuinely happy to see me; his smile said as much. It had been a while since .... No use getting too far ahead.

"Yes, that's me. JK."

"So, what can I get you?"

His dancing eyes hinting much was on offer.

"A Coke, please."

I needed simple. The basics would do well.

"Sure thing. I was about to close for the night, but there's no rule against serving you a soda. Have a seat. I'll be right back."

He had an admirable backside. Sizzle, sizzle.

"Nice shoes," he said.

"Well, it's the overall outfit that counts."

Was I even a bit sexy?

"You know, I think it's the overall woman that counts."

He stroked his chin just then, toying with me.

Too much.

"I'll take the Coke to go."

Time to run away. Legs came in handy that way. It wasn't entirely fair to confuse him. Say something else, JK.

"Thanks, though. For staying open and all."

He smarted back; rejection was not the norm for a guy like that.

"Anytime you're thirsty, JK, Just stop in. I'll be here."

Good of him.

"Just show yourself out. I'll lock up in a bit."

More of that backside. I left him in my rearview mirror.

Chapter 7

Road Trip Part 1, A Reunion

Dad was good about lending me the car. The keys were on the kitchen table early that morning, along with Mom's home-brew wafting through all the way to my room upstairs. A magnet of sorts.

They were sitting at opposite ends of the table when I walked in. No banter, no chitchat. Being in the same room had to count for something, though. Dad looked up from the table with nothing more that day than his usual morning expression as he considered the day ahead. It was the same look Susie, and I got every morning back before he lost his daughter, back when the world was still a friendly place for us all.

"Full up, JK. You should be fine for the day."

"Have some cereal, dear. I left a couple of boxes out for you. The milk is in the fridge, of course." Mom chimed in, still looking after the kid.

"Thanks, Mom. Thanks, Dad."

I took my place at the table between them with my coffee and cereal bowl.

"Where are you going?"

They spoke in unison! I wish they had waited for me to have at least some of the coffee.

"I'm going out with . . ."

Well, now here was a problem: who was Francine? My very own grief buddy? A strange French lady? A woman with a story? I chose the most straightforward description.

"A friend. I'm going with a friend."

"Who?" Mom this time.

"You don't know her."

"Well, dear, when you're ready, we'd love to meet her. For tea, perhaps?"

Mom waited for more. She wasn't patient usually.

"Or dinner even. Whatever you girls like."

I couldn't say much to that. No way Francine was a girl except in her story. I had a feeling I would hear more of the story today. I also was pretty sure Mom wouldn't like her. Nope, two queens do not a pair make.

"Sure, Mom. Sure."

I took my cue to exit, caffeine-less and with only two spoon-fuls of the cereal.

"Be safe, JK." Dad this time, practical as ever.

I headed to the car and sat in the driver's seat. My last ride with Susie had been in this car; chemo was over, and the verdict was in. We were getting her results.

"Only JK" had been Susie's decision for that ride.

Mom and Dad stood on the porch, waving goodbye a bit madly as if their two girls were heading on some fantastic voyage. They weren't entirely wrong. We were on a journey with strangers holding Susie's lifeblood in their hands, torturing my body through hers. Susie's latter-day brethren, the white coats, had been sure at first when presenting the treatment plan. But all that certainty just led us to the cemetery.

"I don't think more treatment will help. It's time to make you comfortable."

The white coat made his pronouncement quickly. No preliminaries. It was a well-rehearsed tactic. A brief pause completed the scene before an "I'm sorry," coupled with a sad, sympathetic smile.

My sister only said, "Thank you."

Then, straight as a rod, she stood up, smoothed her dress, and shook the white coat's hand. I was sure her grip was still firm. I left right behind her. Dejected. Uncertain of what came next. At least Susie knew enough to get the hell out.

Then the silent drive home. We had no heart for conversation. A block from the house, Susie finally spoke.

"Pull over, JK."

No time to argue. The tires screeched, and the car hit the curb. We were held back by the seatbelts, both a bit breathless.

"Susie?"

She looked at me, traveling some great distance back into

the car from where her thoughts had taken her.

"It will be quick now. I'd like it to be quick."

"Susie?" I was getting good at redundancy.

"JK, you know what I'd like?"

"Tell me."

And what I couldn't say out loud.

"Tell me anything Susie, anything good, anything white, anything shiny, anything beautiful. Tell me the worst. Tell me your nightmares. Don't be alone. I'm here, Susie. I'm here. Tell me what to do."

She did.

"I'd like us to go to the park. You know, Stanford Park? Remember? I think we could get ourselves into some of the kiddie swings. Can we go there now, please?"

"The park?"

She surprised me.

"I just want to remember, JK. Just remember that time …."

And the park it was, the two of us swinging wildly.

We fit. Just.

Looks from the nannies and the moms didn't bother us. We were ourselves, the twins from Holland Drive, new to the neighborhood—little girls. Bright, beautiful girls, Mom always told us. The whole world was ours. What other lies had she told us, our warrior Mom? None, Susie said. Not lies. Her hopes. She told us all that was possible.

Oh, yes, we went swinging after the white coats were through with us. *"Hang on, Susie! Hang on!"*

I stepped back out of the car. My breathing was caught up in the memory of the swings and took a while to come back to me. I wiped my sweaty palms on the thighs of my black jeans. My hands took some time to stop shaking.

I had Susie's bright red sweater, Missoni. A little thin for the crisp weather. That was why my whole body was cold, right? I headed back into the house for my leather jacket, hoping my dashing pace would avoid my running into either Mom or Dad. Up past the pictures. I grabbed the coat and then down past the photos. Which picture was the right one for our swinging years? Which one?

I stopped cold. Dashing was no longer imperative. Ah, yes. There it was. The picture with the family in front of the house. All of us. Susie and I were grinning between Mom and Dad. We had just moved in. Fashion aside, we were picture perfect. Perfect in that snap of a moment. Isn't everyone allowed a moment like that?

I slowed down. With the jacket now on my back, my mind returned to the present. It was time to continue.

"Go, JK. You can go now."

I don't know who said that, but I obeyed the voice.

My hands were steady again. The car moved out of the driveway smoothly. Dad stared out from his office window, Mom from her upstairs bedroom window. Both looked away as I looked back at the house, in unison, yet separate.

Picture perfect. It told a story.

Francine was in her new outfit, the brown tweed suit, with Susie's shawl tightly wound around her slim frame. The hat was nowhere in sight. She seemed smaller without it, almost human size. I was wrapped up in memories of Susie the whole drive over to the cemetery until I saw Francine; the simple fact of her figure called me to the present. I stepped out of the car and opened the door for her. I even closed it after she took Susie's spot in the passenger seat.

She was taut.

"Good morning, JK."

"Good morning. I brought some coffee for us." In the console between us, the Dunkin' travel mugs were a solid presence.

"Oh, thank you. And for the ride. I do so appreciate it."

So proper.

"Sure."

Less proper.

Which of us was more real?

"So, where are we going?"

"Here, I wrote down the address."

Her hand shook as she handed me the slip of paper. It was way outside of town—time for the technology to kick in. I gasped when the GPS indicated it would be a two-hour drive up north to wine country. Well, now I understood why the lady needed a ride.

"OK, let's go."

I was going with her, this mysterious French woman. Going away from my memories, away from the cemetery.

We were quiet for most of the drive. I kept her involved in the navigation, pointing out the city limits and the small towns I knew as we drove on to the mystery location. Even the sight of the Golden Gate Bridge didn't impress my passenger; she was in a world of her own. Soon enough, we were in the Napa Valley, where small, tidy vines were trussed up in tight rows. The coffee dictated a biological pause. Lucky for us, this was a friendly part of the state, and we were shown to a lady's room at the first picnic stop. When we got back into the car after the short stop, I had to say something.

"Just a half-hour now to Calistoga."

"A half-hour," she murmured right back. "Oh, my. So close."

She clutched the wrap. I glanced over. Her eyes were closed. I thought I could see pain on her face.

"So, what is in this place we're going to?"

"The real question is *who*. Who is in this place? Maybe no one. Maybe nothing."

"Doesn't seem like nothing."

"You are right, JK." She paused for a moment. "It's all of it, really. All of it."

She turned away from me, staring at the scenery, her hand still at her chest.

Small talk? More serious talk? I was undecided.

She continued. "You know, it was my fault. I was young. A

silly girl. But I often wonder if I knew what I was doing anyway."

"Kids don't usually understand much."

I needed to help her along.

"Children in that time and in that place grew up much faster than what you experienced, my dear girl."

I was anything but "dear girl." Her tone was cutting. She was sharp enough now. Something about getting closer to this place, to the person she was going to see. I had a guess now as to whom it was.

"I'm sorry, JK. It's the memories. Of that time and of what came after."

She touched my arm as if to make up. What was this between us anyway?

"What happened exactly?"

There. Full-frontal assault.

"I, I . . . ."

Don't speak out loud, JK, quiet now.

"I was a girl. I was not quite innocent enough. It was disastrous. In the end, Judith was one of the shaved women, all because of me."

My mind raced. Shaved women in France. There it was. They were the women who slept with the Nazis. In the backlash and fury of the aftermath of the liberation, they were shamed publicly and banished. Who knew what they deserved? There were no easy answers in such times.

"What did you do?"

Time to get personal.

"I decided I should have a piece of what Judith had. I tried over and over. It didn't work, though. I failed."

Francine's mind headed out of the car to her village in France. Maybe the sight of the vineyards helped her imagine her own country.

"I saw him looking at her. I couldn't tell what was on his mind initially; but I knew he was captivated by my straight, honest, clear-headed sister. Later, I suffered with him. In the end, I triumphed. But not in time for Judith."

She whispered the last words. The girl she had been and the woman she was now had a complicated relationship.

I glanced over at Francine. This was a woman reliving a moment of accomplishment. She had put one over on this man. That much was clear. But, from what she said, both girls were severely hurt. Her sister more so than Francine. Then what? Regret? Pain? Shame?

All the above. As I learned more of her story, I would find out it was all the above, and then some.

We arrived in the town, a touristy wine place but not as affluent as I expected. There were signs for mud baths in rustic spa windows. I could not imagine sitting in a pile of muck willingly. Crazy.

We continued past the center of town, and a few minutes later, the electronic GPS voice announced we had arrived at our destination. I looked at the two-story building. It was an old folks' home of some sort. A pretty shabby one. There was an old fellow in suspenders, mismatched shoes, not too many teeth, holding a shiny cane and sitting on an old park bench by the concrete entrance.

"Howdy, ladies."

The less-than-toothy grin was genuine.

"Good day."

Francine, ever the lady, acknowledged the man with a brief nod of the head and glided past him. The small glass doors to the building were encased in metal, which scraped the concrete step. A small arc was etched into the step due to the ongoing movement in and out of the building. It made a hell of a noise, worse than any squeaking at our porch door. Francine pulled on the door with both hands to shut it behind her. I was too slow and remained outside.

"Nice day for a visit," the old guy said, looking at me.

"Sure is."

I owed him a bit of a conversation.

"You've not been here before."

The man made a firm statement. I figured he was usually at the door.

"Nope, never been."

"It's a pretty decent place. At least the food isn't too tough to chew." He winked. "So, what brings you here?"

"She does." I nodded in Francine's direction inside the lobby of the building.

"I guess you gotta be pretty quick to keep up with that one. She's a real scamperer, if you know what I mean."

"Gotta go. Good to meet you."

I meant that last one. That old fellow got my first real smile since Susie died. He deserved it. He made it happen.

"Come back anytime. I'm Bill, by the way."

He nodded my way one final time before turning back to his sentinel duties.

I wasn't so sure about following Francine. I stared at the arc on the concrete floor. Finally, I reasoned a two-hour ride was a bit of an investment and decided to go in after her.

"Room 202, you said? Is that correct, two zero two?"

Francine still had a sharpness and was shredding someone else. The young man at the desk was clearly in shock being in front of someone like Francine, and she didn't even have the black hat on. When I came along, he did a double-take. The pair of us were just too much for him with his sensible no-name polo shirt and khaki trousers. I imagined he was the local version of a preppie young man.

"Yyyeesss." I never knew a one-syllable word could be so elongated.

I smiled a little unkindly, but not for long. He was too sweet for the two of us to gang up on him.

"How do we get there?" I asked casually.

No use removing every drop of wit the young fellow might have left.

"Up, I mean, up the stairs. Just there." A slightly shaky hand shot up to point us in the right direction. "And then turn right and right again at the second set of doors, It's at the end of the hallway," he added, seeming more sure of himself.

And off we went. Francine moved slowly. She aged in this place with every step. Smells of disinfectant and oldness were baked into the once-flowery walls of the hallways. She was miles away from where she had been a girl.

At the door, she came to a complete stop. Her hand went up to knock just above the "Bienvenue" vintage welcome sign on the worn door with paint flaking in the corners with the older dark color showing through a light beige topcoat.

Darkness covered by light, a little trite in terms of symbolism. Movies are all around us. It wasn't the first time I figured that out, but it hit me in the face just the same.

Francine knocked. She threw her shoulders back. The door opened. She leaned in, eyes open, intent on pressing forward.

The sign gave it away. I knew who she had come to see. The rest, however, would be a revelation.

Dad had been wrong. Not quite enough gas. We stopped at a gas station close to the city so that I could fill up for him on the way home.

I watched Francine buckle into herself as a trucker spat onto the ground next to the gas pump. She shuddered, personally offended by such a crass display of bodily function. Yet, every aspect of the trip, even this, was an illumination of human nature.

I stared at the spatter with an uneasy feeling of empathy for the expelled liquid as it congealed on the cold ground.

Spatter in tatters.

"Nice day, honey?" Mom spoke first.

She and Dad were sitting on the couch in the living room. On the same sofa! And me: where did I belong? I ended up on the love seat opposite them.

"Not sure. No. I wouldn't say it was nice."

Seminal, dramatic, unexpected: yes. Nice? No.

Mom looked at me, a barrage of questions on the tip of her tongue when Dad came to the rescue.

"So, the car held up OK for you?" he said.

"Sure did. Thanks, Dad. I filled it up for you."

I tried to swat the image of the spit away. I didn't want it near Dad; he might not be able to shoo it away on his own.

"Patrice, see, I told you. Nothing to worry about." He was getting bold, moving the warrior back to allow the fledgling some room. Maybe I was getting Dad back. The Dad Susie and I had when we were little.

"Now, what shall we do about dinner? Patrice, how about I take you both out tonight? What do you say?"

Had he even said that many words in one breath since Susie died?

Mom was slow to catch up. She looked at me and sized up the depth of my discomfort. Mom then looked over to my Dad to evaluate his resolve. The calculation concluded after one more look at each of us. The arithmetic must have made sense to her.

"Well, Roger, I don't think I want to be out in public. I have a roast in the fridge we can have if you two will just give me an hour. Why don't you go outside for a bit?"

Mom made her position clear. She was, however, gentler than expected.

It wasn't long until my Dad had me talking on the porch. Had he always been such a good listener? Susie would have been surprised. Or maybe not. That night I figured out there was a lot about Dad he kept to himself. I would learn it all over again in a few weeks.

By the time Mom called us in, Dad had a pretty good idea about Francine. He just said, "People do surprising things. But JK, some time to yourself wouldn't be so bad. You've got a lot to figure out."

"Yeah, maybe."

In saying what happened with Francine, I realized there was a lot she had not shared. What she had shown me was not pretty.

"Let's go in. No need to push our luck."

"Right, Dad. After you."

"No, sweetheart, we'll go in together."

And with my father's arm around my shoulder, we squeezed through the door to where my mother waited.

Chapter 8

Women's Stories

I woke up in my old room, comforted by the cozy blanket and the childhood memories all around. Before even brushing my teeth, I had my laptop out to capture a jumble of notes. As I worked on getting the women's stories into better shape, I thought of Francine and Judith and their remarkable past. I was not ready to write anything about those two women yet. Their place was in the background as I processed words about the women from Mom's group. The keyboard came alive, like their stories. I felt hopeful I could make something of this. I tucked my own emotions away so the heat of the stories could rise. I ignored the strain in my back and shoulders in a mad attempt to get at the core of the women. I started with Emily's story.

Emily looked up, her face awash in tears and snot, the pitiful Kleenex in her hand now a wet ball. She had told all.

Her intentions were formed that morning as she scrubbed herself clean in the shower. She would not keep quiet again. Three group meetings without a word from her lips were enough. It was time. She knew it from the moment she was drying off. She kept her resolve from the shower to the group meeting and rushed to be the first to speak.

"My name is Emily. My son, Timmy, died. He was hit by a car as he ran after our dog in the street. Our neighbor saw it. I just heard her scream. He was five. It was a lovely service. The entire family flew in. Stayed with us for a week. It was helpful to have them nearby. Now it's just my husband and me. We're a bit broken. Not sure that I care anymore, though."

In truth, Emily spoke to herself. In the room, she had stopped talking after the word "died." The other women had waited, knowing their patience might coax more from her.

One of the women across from her, the one with the shabby outfit and the square jaw, opened her mouth ever so slightly. Emily tried to remember her name. Kate, yes. Her name was Kate. Kate was about to exhale. Was she going to say a sympathetic word or two? No. Kate closed her mouth before a single word came out. Only her breath left a trace. So fragile it might stop at any moment. Just like that. No more. Emily stopped at "died." She might always stop there, just like her life.

Kate looked at the proper young woman sitting across from her. She was going to say something. It had taken her several meetings, two or three maybe, to gather her courage. She finally spoke and said her name was Emily. Son, dead. Well, they all had a death. That's why they were in the group. The string of pearls around Emily's frail neck made Kate cringe. She usually disliked that kind of affectation, especially under the circumstances. Kate was just about to murmur some-thing about that to herself when Emily looked straight at her from across the room. Emily had gone quiet, unable to say more. Kate closed her mouth. No, she couldn't judge the pearls after the tears started spilling out. Dear me, she thought. This one has a way to go.

Writing about the core of the women was a hot, scary place. Beautiful too. I would work on that with my keyboard.

Mom came to the door with a loud knock. The words stopped streaming from my fingers. Mom's head angled in the doorway, then more of her body as she stepped into the room. She had her makeup on and one of her lovely cardigans, cream color. Only her yoga pants betrayed an anomaly in her dress.

Her heart was another matter—seriously uncharted territory, at least for me.

"JK, I am making some coffee and a snack. Would you like some?"

A hopeful half-smile, a slight hesitation. "Your Dad had to go out for a bit. It's just you and me."

"Sounds great, Mom. I'll be right down."

Against all odds, I smiled at the sudden interruption, thankful for my mother's genuine self. She looked surprised and then happy I had said yes.

"Great! Five minutes, Josephine."

She was still running the show. I grinned even more. It didn't take long for me to close the laptop. I copied the document on my flash drive. Double save everything. Every writer knows that. Double save.

Susie and I: double with no save. Not yet. I was working on it.

I could make out the aroma of the cinnamon coffee-cake Mom had addicted us to while we grew up. Susie and I fought epic battles over every morsel. Mom always smiled knowingly at Dad whenever Susie and I got into it over the cake portions. He would smile right back at us and at her, enveloping us. Susie and I never noticed their collusion—or at least I thought I didn't notice. But the images must have been captured, waiting for the day of their release. It was upon us now. Oh, don't be so dramatic, JK. Just eat the damn cake.

I was still in my pajamas when Mom and I sat at the kitchen table. We were an unlikely pair.

"Oh dear, I forgot the napkins. Would you mind?"

"No problem, Mom."

Some unnamed energy force was with me. I even did a little dance on the way back to the table. It seemed all it took was a little writing!

"Oh, JK. My, my. You are in a good mood. I'm happy to see it. Is it the writing? I noticed the laptop was getting quite the workout this morning."

She started on the coffeecake even without the napkin. I should have sensed then something was not right.

"I have a few ideas starting to come together."

"Can you talk about it?"

"Not yet. It's not done. I can say you were part of the inspiration."

My habit was to keep my work close to the vest, just in case things didn't pan out. Writers never know where they might end up. Even the best start can lead you to a whole lot of nothing.

"That's good, I suppose. Nothing nasty about me, eh dear? I couldn't bear it!" Mom's voice cracked just then. She regrouped quickly. "Any other inspirations?"

"All of it. It's all coming together."

And it was, each piece around me connecting into the next. I hoped I could make it work.

"Good."

Basic words can mean so much.

The cake was enormously satisfying, and the coffee managed to enhance the energy that started with the writing that morning. I waited for more. I wanted more. Insatiable. I had high hopes for Mom and me.

Some misguided confidence made me take the plunge.

"Mom, what's going on with you?"

"Honey, why would you ask something like that?"

Shifting herself in the chair, Mom looked away from me.

"Look, you wanted to talk the other day. I'm here. Mom, I'm right here. So, let's talk."

The words were more forceful than I anticipated. They pried something loose.

"I can't get past this, JK. It's just not possible. And now, now . . . ."

No tears, just a vacant look.

"What? Mom. Look at me. What's wrong?"

"I need to leave, JK. Get away. At least for a while."

I was stunned.

"You're running away?"

No more filters; it just came out.

"That's not like you. You're a fighter."

I clenched my fists, whereas her hands—the ones that chopped, patted, dismissed, and comforted—were now still. Inactive. Empty.

A sadness came over her, a hurt from so deep it took time to come to the surface. Her words were measured. "No, sweetheart. I fought because your father didn't, at least not in a way

I could recognize. He's there for you now, though, better than I could be, eh?"

Mom never shied away from the truth; it was part of her fundamental courage.

"Mom, what are you talking about?"

The primal urge to connect with my mother replaced the blunt edge of my earlier happiness. Elation morphed into desperation. I needed her.

"Your sister. No getting over that. The loss of a child, JK, it's astonishing. So much of me was wrapped up in you girls. I never realized until now how unhealthy . . . ."

Mom was lost in her inner world, processing thoughts and feelings. She shared only a fraction. By the time she continued, my fist was an opened palm waiting for the coin.

"I smothered you both. I lost myself somewhere in the process. So boring. Many mothers have the same story, you know."

She held her hand out but couldn't quite reach me. Her words covered the remaining distance.

"Strange how I thought I was doing so much good for the world just because of the two of you."

Her eyes were vacant. It's the silent sobs you need to worry about. I was petrified.

"Mom, you know, it wasn't that bad."

"JK, will you be honest with me?" She leaned over the table, slightly out of her chair, and grabbed my hand, squeezing it hard. "Were you and Susie happy? I mean, as kids growing up, were you happy?"

Her eyes bore into me. Afraid. Anxious.

A moment of universal truth comes along once in a life-time—until it's repeated. This was a first for us: mother and daughter, nothing else. Truth *is* a dare.

"We were, Mom. Happy. Full. Susie and I had a good child-hood. The best."

The deep sigh from Mom opened a chasm I could never bridge. My view of childhood contained Susie larger than life; she was all I could see of it. I never considered Mom's or Dad's role in making it happen. Selfish, awkward, and plain dumb. I was wretched.

"Thank you."

And there it was, a mother's love, relief, and grace inter-twined. She rose at that moment. Regal. No other word for it.

She had packed her bags some time ago. A retreat, she said. To find herself. I hoped she would not be lost forever; I had only just started to find my way to her. Then, at the front door came a few more words from her.

"Don't worry, JK. It will be fine someday. You, me, your father. I know it will."

Dad? I had forgotten him.

"Oh, he and I already spoke, dear. We said our goodbyes earlier. I asked him to give us some time alone so we could talk. You look after yourself."

I went into her embrace. Solace at last. Brief. My arms were empty too quickly. But I knew where to go for human contact.

Chapter 9

False Start

I headed over to the bar and to Patrick. It was foolish, but the man just called to me. It was so early in the day that no one else would be there. Sure enough, he was alone, readying for another day of the worst of human nature on display. I used to be that display for many such Patricks—none of them quite as tantalizing as the current one in front of me.

"JK. Great to see you again."

The lusty brown eyes caught mine. He had to know what was on my mind, at least in as much as it concerned him.

"Hey, Patrick." I smiled.

I wore one of my red-light, booty-call outfits: a tight black halter-top with slick leather pants. The leather jacket had come off already; I hung it on one of the stools. It felt good to be on the prowl again. The cold air in the bar made my nipples erect, which his eyes took in as soon as I moved closer to him.

"You look great."

He course-corrected and looked straight into my eyes. Honey.

How soon until he might lick my shoulder? Now, please. What's wrong with now? I sat on one of the stools midway up the length of the bar.

"Thanks. You, too. You look good."

No need to be subtle in this game.

"A Coke?"

He moved towards the back, still on the other side of the long wooden bar.

"Sure."

I swiveled halfway around on the stool I had only just started to occupy and jumped off. I moved towards the man, leaving all else behind. I followed Patrick up my side of the bar, training a finger behind me on the smooth surface, hips swaying at the thought of what would come next.

"I'd like to see where you keep it."

He turned around at the sound of my voice so close to him. He was surprised but regained his composure quickly. One more check next to his name. Nothing yet in the negative column. This guy could be good.

"Right this way, ma'am. I'll show you where I keep things."

He took me in and grinned back at me.

"Come on. It's all in the backroom. Watch your step. I haven't yet washed the floor; it will be slick in spots."

Doubtless, other females trailed this man, smelling as I did a sweet, naughty sexiness that promised delights of all sorts. I hoped he would have his clothes off in the next ten minutes. Slickness was on my mind. The floor would do fine.

He bent over to reach into the bottom of his industrial refrigerator.

"It's going to be back in here somewhere. Hang on a sec."

No more hanging on for me. I went over to him and put my hands on his hips, caressed the side of his legs, hung a thumb off the back pocket of his jeans, and caressed his ass cheek. I was right up against him; there was no mistaking my intentions.

"Wow! Oh!"

He turned around. The taut muscles of his arms went straight to my back for an oddly shy embrace. He hugged me. Oh no, this would not do.

"Hey, Patrick. What do you say we skip the preliminaries and get to it?"

Unusually blunt, even for me. He gave me a long look. I read him as dazed and intrigued—but holding back. I had to work for my prize. I stepped out from his embrace and took his hand to my breast. His eyes widened, then closed.

He came to me.

Before long, our tongues met, and I had my hands on his belt buckle to strip him of that impediment. He was rock hard. Good boy. His hand reached from my breast to my navel and back to my ass, which he squeezed and then slid his hand through my legs. The shock of it made me coo out loud.

"Yes, yes."

I started to take off my leather pants, but he held my hands back.

"Let me."

He turned me around, up against the wall, kicking the crates on the ground away from us. One hand still cruised down my front while the other held both of mine up against the wall. His tongue ravaged my ear and neck. He was right up against me, hard and smooth. I buckled back into him. My nipples jumped to life under his touch, and I could barely hold my hips still. They arched back to meet his pelvis and his shaft.

"Now. Come on. Now."

I couldn't wait. I jimmied my way free of the wall and my hands back down onto my pants to take them off. I was operating on instincts. The promise of sex clouded all rational thought. I had come looking for contact, and I was going to get it.

"Woman, stop. Hey! What's this all about?"

His voice broke through the frenzy in my mind.

I tore myself away, out of the space we created into the cold, drab back room of the bar. I looked around me and then finally at the man I had practically assaulted. Patrick stood firm. He might just be that exceptional man who declared himself unwilling to play the counterpart to my single-minded, sex-seeking woman-on offer role.

"What? You're not interested?"

The words stumbled out. Switched off from the sex, the wildness drained itself into one big knot in my chest.

Breathless, his chest heaved as well. His words were choppy.

"That's not it, JK. I am very interested in *you*. But not in *this*. Can you slow down just a bit?"

Slow down? No. That was not the scene I was after. I wanted blinding quick sex and then my exit. Angry as hell, I just took the exit.

A few blocks away, it was just me in my ridiculous outfit on the sidewalk with the rest of the trash that had accumulated. Above me, a cool, bright sky reminded me how small I was in the world. I wish I had my leather jacket, but I had left it behind in Patrick's bar when I ran out.

"Susie, Susie, Susie. It's not supposed to be this hard."

My fists clenched again. I sat on the hard, cold concrete, more alone now that I had been so close to the whirl of passion and sex. An empty urban landscape looked back, mocking me. My sister would have asked me more gently: "What did you expect?"

Our last real conversation about men had been before the start of Susie's chemo.

"I gave Jack back his ring."

"What! Why? Susie, why? He's crazy about you."

"JK, I think it's easier this way. For all of us."

"Huh? I don't get it, Suze. It's for better or worse, isn't it?"

"That's after the marriage vows, JK."

"That bastard. He should be with you."

"He didn't have a choice, JK. I don't want him now."

"I don't understand you, Susie."

"Oh, JK. Don't you see? I want to be me until the last moment. I can't do that with Jack around. He's just too honest. He's like a mirror. Anyway, it's not his decision. It's mine."

Susie was right. Jack was honest. He was a perfect match to her spirit. A young lawyer, public defendant, crusader, and lover. I had not been prepared to like him, he, who would have my sister; but he won me over with his easy manner. A straightforward guy you could count on. At least that was what Mom said. Dad added, "A good man, Susie."

Then, hugs all around. It would be a small wedding, Susie had said. So small it ultimately vanished.

"So, what? He just accepted it, and left you? Some guy."

I kicked the air. Was nothing solid?

"JK, it's just you and me. Jack, well, he's not going to be there. Wasn't meant to be."

That single tear down her face snapped me back out of my childish anger, right back to her side where I belonged, always and forever.

On the sidewalk, in my ridiculous outfit, I wiped my own tear. The sun was still out but did little to warm me.

"There you are."

Against all odds, it was Patrick with my jacket. He handed it to me, blocking the sun for a moment until he sat down next to me.

"OK, if I keep you company?"

Yes, OK, and then some. I smiled at him, a small, crooked half-smile. He smiled back with no reservation and put his arm around me while I calmed the raging spirits.

"Susie, here I go. No more games. But it's hard. Courage now. Just like Mom. Courage."

"Lunch?"

His smooth hand stroked my tear away and brushed my hair back.

"Why?"

I had so many questions for this hunk of a man, who came chasing down the wanton version of the grieving sister and lost child without knowing any of it.

"Because I'm hungry. Are you?"

Those brown eyes. Bloody hell, I was in trouble. Maybe it was the long womanly lashes or that sensuous mouth of his.

"Seriously. Why?"

Answer please. I needed at least one answer.

"It's those outfits. Can't wait to see what's next."

He grinned. He had me then. Clever boy.

"Oh, right. Sure."

"Come on."

Patrick was up in a flash, holding his hand out to me. I put mine right into his. This was the touch for me. Against all odds I had found it. He pulled me up with one firm motion.

"I'm a mess."

I owed him a direct warning in case the assault and my current state did not speak loudly enough on my behalf.

"I know."

He dropped a short peck on my dry lips.

"We all are. Come on," he insisted again. "I really am hungry, and I need to open by three today."

"Only if you know a good burger joint."

I needed to be back in familiar territory.

"A meat-eater. Love it. Let's go, JK."

"Let's go then."

It turned out Patrick did know a good burger joint. It was a breezy sort of lunch with the kind of dialogue you don't write ahead of time. I said yes right away when he asked for a date on his one night off, Sunday. I had several days to prepare for it.

"No messy wantonness this time, Susie."

"Promise?"

"Yes, I promise. I promise not to start there anyway." Wink.

A few hours later, I was back at Susie's grave. I hoped I wouldn't run into Francine. This was not her time. It was my time. Mine and Susie's. Time for a heart to heart with my sister, even if I had to imagine her side of the dialogue.

"Dunno, Sis. It's pretty wild here."

I couldn't sit. I talked as I paced around her headstone.

"Yeah, I know. The outfit, not much to it, eh? What? You say it might attract a bad sort of fella? Oh, Susie, I was the bad one. No, no booze. No drugs either. I just sort of, well, I went all sex-crazed psycho on the guy. But he's OK. Patrick's pretty OK."

"No! You know the rule, no talking about men. No details unless there is something worth saying. So, more on that later,

after our date. Yes, a proper date."

"Did you know Mom's gone for a bit on her own? She told me over coffeecake. Remember the coffeecake? No, I don't know how long."

"How's Dad? Well, I haven't spoken to him. Well, hang on, we did talk last night. That was one heck of a day. Was Dad always good to talk to?"

I was all out of news.

"Suze, I miss you. I wish you were here. You and Mom both say we'll be OK. I don't get how you can both be so sure of that."

"Hey, wait. Have you and Mom been talking too?"

Chapter 10

With Father

Dad was home, on the porch when I came home. Lucky for me, he had always seen past my costumes straight into his daughter. "So, you know about your Mom?"

"Yeah, we talked this morning, just before she left."

"I'm sorry. I know it's hard on you."

My dad's first thought was for my loss; his own came second. It was one heck of a lesson in parental love. Mom, and now Dad, forever teaching me.

"What about you, Dad?"

His wife was gone. Surely, he was the primary concern.

"Ah. You know, JK, your mother is a complicated woman. I can't hold her back. Never could. Never tried, actually. A woman like that needs all her space. That's my job. Making space happen for her."

"I thought she was pushing you away."

"May have looked that way, but I couldn't have her pushing on anything. No, I couldn't have that. I took the hint early on."

"Hint?"

"Oh, you know. If you pay any kind of attention, you'll see your Mom likes to have things her way."

That playful wink was back along with a short laugh.

"Remarkable, my Patrice. Remarkable."

He was lost in love, after all this time. After all of this, he loved her. Wow. I was knocked back by his quiet endurance. My Dad was some man.

"I've been a lucky man, JK, to love a woman like your mother. And to have two beautiful girls like you and Susie. Ah, there she is, our Susie. I can still see her, JK. You notice how she's everywhere?"

I didn't speak. It was my turn to listen.

Dad kept talking, his low baritone was deeper than ever.

"Did you know she could never drive a stick shift? She wanted to do that Doctors Without Borders thing, but the stick stood in her way. So talented in every other way. I could never figure it out. I thought the girl would strip every gear in Harry's truck. I had to tell her to give up. Not sure she ever forgave me. Harry either, for that matter."

Good old Harry, our neighbor of twenty years plus. A bit hairy for Susie and me, but a good sort of fella.

Dad was a keeper of secrets. I had never seen it. All those assumptions. Time to ask a little something directly.

"Dad? Why now? Why are you telling me all this now?"

"You should know it all. You should know what's in your father's heart, JK."

My father. I was the lucky one. He stuck by me. First Susie, now him. I reckoned he had been there all along, in that remote way of his. Right there, all along. Whew.

"Is it too much, JK?"

"Too much, Dad? Never too much."

"Susie, we never got it, Sis. Never got him."

"Come on. We have to figure out dinner. I can make an omelet. At least I could before I met your mother."

"I can toast!"

"Excellent. That's just the ticket, kid. Come with me."

The dinner was a mess. I loved it.

I held Francine and her wicked story on the fringe while I got on writing about Mom's women for the next little while. The familiar rush was back. I recognized it quickly enough, even though it had been many years. The words flowed; the images made sense. It was real. I was giddy. Click, click, click for hours at a time. The women's stories weaved one into the other until I managed to make their circle careen back into itself. Gentle writing was the way for the women. They looped and threaded back onto themselves through my keyboard until I made their stories unbreakable.

Would I be able to manage a happy ending? Susie loved happy endings. She would have said, "Why not, JK?" Susie wasn't a writer, but she knew how to get through, at least to me.

"Well, Sis, I don't know yet. I just don't know where this one is going."

Dad kept me company in the house through the days. He went to his office right after breakfast. Through the open door, I could see him, intent and happy at his desk, while I sat with the laptop on the infamous couch. We stayed in tune with each other this way, at a distance.

Something about the ties that bind us to family, even the cliché, was a comfort. I still didn't know what he was up to.

"Something about doing some good in this world, JK," was his only response whenever I asked.

We sat together for each meal but got smarter about getting takeout for dinner and avoiding any cooking. Dad would head out an hour or so before dinner and come back with the goodies. Our chitchat was comfortable talk, nothing too deep. No need to say what we both knew. He still used the cot.

"Got used to it by now, JK," he explained.

I accepted that and all other answers at face value. Fashioned on his own example with Mom, I gave him space.

Guilt loomed over the two of us at the easiness in our arrangement. Yet, the new world order suited us. Two: that number worked for Dad and me. At least for a few days.

I wish we had snapped a picture for the wall.

Sunday came. Time for my date with Patrick, a second chance of sorts. I had all of Susie's wardrobe out. Like a real girl, I took my time before the final selection. In the end, I donned a pair of skinny designer jeans, a flowing top with embroidery (very seventies) with a camisole underneath (more classy than last time), and killer sexy wedge sandals (though no painted toenails). I grabbed a long cardigan for later when it would get chilly. I was a walking contradiction of sweetness and daring.

"Perfect," Dad said, looking up from the paper. "Have fun, sweetheart."

He even gave me a kiss on the cheek and a pat on my arm. He had asked a few fatherly questions about "this fellow" ever since I had mentioned the date. What could I tell him other than the name of the bar where I met Patrick? There were some things a father should not know.

Patrick waited for me at a café near the bar. I rode the bus to the café. He stood up as soon as I came through the door. He wore a pair of dusty old Levi's with a weathered leather belt and a print cotton shirt with multiple tiny flowers in shades of green. He wasn't afraid of style, nor did he exaggerate. He looked scrumptious. Good times ahead.

"You look great, JK!"

Twinkles and a smile greeted me.

"You have a habit of saying that."

A wit of my own; I had my mojo back.

"JK, you make it so damned easy on a guy."

A laugh. Patrick had his own way with humor.

"Would you like to head out? I have my car around the corner. I thought we could drive up to Foothills Park. I picked up a picnic before you got here."

He held up a paper bag full of groceries in one hand and a bottle of wine in the other.

Foothills Park was a reserve outside the city and home to make-out hopefuls from all over the area. Folks had to show proof of residency at the gate, so it was never busy. Once in, you could easily find a spot in the beautiful park where no one would disturb you.

"Mmmm, sure, Patrick. Sounds good."

The truth was I didn't care where we went, but I was touched he had put so much thought into it. We were lucky it was a warmer day than most for late October. We would still need to generate some kind of heat in the great outdoors.

I held the door to the café open for him as he had his hands full. If luck was on my side, those hands of his would soon . . . no more of that. Second chances; remember, JK?

Duly self-chastised, I followed him to his car, trying for the innocent—repeat, only innocent thoughts. It was tough.

Patrick had an easy, graceful walk.

I was a few paces behind as he called out, "Here we go. Your carriage, my lady."

He stopped by a vintage 1964 Mercedes convertible, white with cream interior.

"It used to be my mom's," he said shyly.

Was he apologizing for the color? The man was full of surprises.

I got into the car beside the hunk.

"Susie, I am going for a ride. Up to the hills where the city gives way to the forest, up against the sky."

The heater was blasting and kept us warm for the short drive from town, past the Stanford campus, into the park itself. Patrick was a smooth driver. The car was too sexy for anything else.

Patrick and I had laid out the food together, and he uncorked the wine bottle.

"So, what's your story, JK?" he asked.

"Story?"

So many stories, all wound together, even this scene.

"Yeah, what brings you to this place?"

"I thought it was your mom's white Mercedes?"

Would he fall for that one? On the ride over, I learned his mom had recently moved to the East Coast, New York, where a car like that one just wouldn't do well. "You keep it here, Patrick," she had told him. She must be one classy lady, I imagined. The only thing I knew for sure is that she must be a great mother; her son smiled when he spoke of her. Had Susie and I ever been that good to our mother?

"Funny lady. You let me know when you want to share."

No sign of impatience. He must have decided he had all the time in the world.

I watched his throat as he swallowed more of the wine and looked at the city's vista at our feet. I did not touch the glass he poured for me. I stared at the lickety-split handsome fella I sat next to. How much would I give him? Facts would be a start.

With a dry swallow of my own, I began.

"I grew up here. We moved here when my sister and I were about six. We had a great childhood. Dad was an engineer; Mom stayed at home."

Was that enough?

"So, you stayed here? I mean, did you ever move away?"

"I was—away—for a while. Berkeley and then Hollywood for a few years."

Gulp; out with it.

"Rehab."

There. So what.

Compassion met my gaze.

"That explains the first night. I should have guessed. I'm sorry."

He added somewhat more brightly, "At least I thought to bring us some water, too!"

He poured me that and took my untouched wine back to himself.

"Yeah, it was pretty awful. But Susie—that's my sister—Susie was there. Never let me go. Not that I made that easy on her."

"She sounds great."

"Yeah."

I didn't want to get into the tenses about Susie is great or was great. So I sucked in some air and decided to redirect the conversation back to him.

"And you? Your family?"

"Boring stuff. Mom is a journalist, always chasing the bad guys. She's got a style of her own."

He drifted off for a moment into his memories. I could respect that.

"Dad, well, he's off with his new wife. He's still around here, but we don't see all that much of each other."

"Why?"

"I guess I was none too understanding when he took up with another woman. Younger, of course. He thought I should be happy for him. He said I couldn't understand just how hard being with Mom had been on him. He could never measure up, or some such. I didn't want to hear about it. I was angry for a while."

Patrick still looked mildly angry to me for a few seconds, though it didn't take him long to clear that out.

"Anyway, it's just as well. Mom got an offer she couldn't refuse, and she's been in New York for the past five years. I miss her, though."

"And now?"

"Now, I have my own life to worry about."

He looked right into me. I looked right back. He threw the ball back into my zone.

"And what do you do to keep busy, JK?"

Apart from improperly grieving for the sister I couldn't save, even though I owed her everything, and being a half-hearted daughter to two parents who are trying their best to cope with her death and my imperfections?

The obvious answer came.

"I'm a writer."

"Anything I would know?"

I gave him the name of my TV series, and he blinked.

"That was you? Wow! I have to say I'm impressed."

"Thanks." I blushed. "I'm going in another direction now."

"And we'll see it on the screen?"

"No, it's a book. I think. Well, I'm not sure yet what it will be."

"I understand."

He probably did understand, I thought.

We worked through the food quietly for a while. Passing the cheese and the baguette at regular intervals. Were the French everywhere? Soon it was all crumbs, and the wine bottle was half empty. His limit, he said.

"So."

"So," I answered back.

And with that, he reached across the feast and kissed me. The softness threw me. He pulled back quickly, but the taste of his lips stayed on mine. I couldn't help but put my fingers up to my mouth.

"Mmmm . . . ."

Oh no! Had I said that out loud?

"JK, I . . . ."

"Stop, Patrick. Stop."

I closed my eyes. Where was this story going? Happy ending or just a wild ride?

"Susie? Do you know? Girl, send me a sign. I can't take it."

"JK?"

Patrick's voice was as soft as that kiss.

"JK? You with me?"

"With you?"

No. Wait. Yes, I want to be.

I drifted off. Colliding images of a delirious Susie and Jack announcing their engagement. A younger version of Mom and Dad laughing at their girls. Susie and I laughing on the swings and other happy memories flooded in.

Stay in the light, JK. Stay in the moment.

"Yes, Patrick, I'm here."

I opened my eyes, looking out, maybe for the first time since we buried Susie.

Patrick reached for me. We sat with me cradled in his arms, watching the world. No words. The heat from Patrick's solid body welded me to him. The heat and that kiss. And the lips, and his sweetness. His hands were strong, moving up and down my arms. He might have been humming in my ear. My eyes were still open, but I couldn't be sure I was taking it all in.

"We'd better head back; it's getting a touch chilly out here."

The voice of reason.

"Already? Alright, then; we'll head back."

Gosh, even his hand was warm. He didn't let go of mine until we reached the car. Time for that cardigan and the heater again.

As we rode back, he wanted to know more and decided to ask about each member of my family as a proxy.

"Dad?"

"A retired engineer."

"Yes, my folks are still together.

"Mom?"

"Oh, she's away for a while."

"Where?"

"A retreat."

"New Agey?"

"No, this agey."

"And your sister?"

"She's still here."

Always here.

He parked the car close to the café. We sat for a bit; it was too soon to quit each other.

"Coffee?" he asked.

"Oh, yes, I could use a cup."

A tall cup of manly tenderness that is.

"Let's go."

As we walked in front of the big window of the coffee shop, I saw an image that knocked me back. Not two steps back, but all the way back. It was true darkness, the kind that comes in a flash, obliterating all else.

Dad sat across from a very attractive lady, blonde, trendy eyeglasses, svelte, in a business suit with a Hermes scarf and three-inch heels. These were the kind of shoes that trample; it was perfect casting. He talked to her, papers in front of him, arms gesticulating. He was more animated and had more life to him than I recalled seeing in him. It was heartbreaking.

Patrick was several steps behind me as I rushed into the shop and just hovered over Dad. The kid-got-caught-with-the-hand-in-the-cookie-jar-look-on-his-face would have been funny if the shoes had not been sitting across from him with alarm spreading over her made-up face. Then guilt—*guilt*—on both their faces. Shit, this was real.

"Dad?"

Yeah, *Dad*, what are you going to say to me, your only daughter? The only one left to accuse him.

"JK! What are you doing here? I thought you were on a date. Oh."

He spied Patrick, who caught up with me and started to extend his hand out to him. I just stormed out, left them both there in a half introduction. It didn't matter to me what Dad thought of Patrick now.

Dad moved quickly and caught up with me outside the shop. This was going to be a bona fide public scene.

"Sorry, JK, I should have told you."

Deplorable, the shame that hung over his shoulder.

"Who is she?"

I was the wounded one; he did not have any rights to that

emotion. No rights at all.

"Jessica? She's an acquaintance."

"Does Mom know?"

"Not in detail. I haven't found the right time to tell her."

"I bet."

The words just seethed out of me.

"It's been difficult. And now, with your mother gone, I can't get away."

Was he looking for my sympathy?

"Stuck, huh? I thought you loved Mom, Dad. Really loved her, understood her. Isn't that what you said to me? All that stuff I just had to know about you?"

"What? Of course, I love Patrice!"

And the man in the street suddenly looked like my Dad again. Like a husband and father, the guy who held us together quietly from the background, the guy who was happy when we were happy. He was throwing it all away!

"Hey, wait, JK. What do you think this is?"

He looked so indignant, confused.

"You tell me, Dad. You tell me."

I turned my back on him. Patrick was right there with me. He heard it all. He understood wayward fathers. We walked away in lockstep. Dad kept calling my name, but it was just a faint echo behind us.

"Take me home, Patrick. Please."

I became old-fashioned and needed a gentleman. My old one let me down.

Patrick led me to his car, to his apartment, and finally to his bed. We slept with our clothes on. He didn't say a word until the following day.

"Talk to him, JK."

"What?"

I was in a daze, having just opened my eyes. Patrick had been awake for a while. I could smell coffee and toast, and he was already dressed. I glanced at the clock. It was already noon.

"Talk to him."

It was a plea from a son to a daughter.

"No."

I was going to talk to someone else.

Patrick kissed me on the forehead. A gentleman.

"The extra keys are on the countertop. Make yourself at home, JK, as long as you want. I'll be back later after I close up at the bar."

Trusting sort of fella. What's not to like about that?

Chapter 11

Wisdom

I waited a good two hours for Francine at the cemetery. My previous concerns about the sun, the clouds, and how to cope were banished in the face of Dad's deception. It was one thing for Susie to up and go; she had no choice. But surely, a family man with Dad's qualities and character could stay faithful to his wife. Why pile on the crap when we were still under the existing heap? I had whipped myself into a froth by the time Francine came over to me.

"Ah, JK, here you are. It's been so long. In a new outfit. Very nice."

"Thanks."

Of course, she would notice my date clothes which I had put back on. She was in her usual black outfit, hat on today, which was my only indication the sun was out, given my frame of mind.

"I'm glad you're here. I was hoping to speak with you."

Francine's mind must be on the trip we had taken together. I didn't want to hear about that and took control of the conversation.

"Why? Why do men lie and cheat?"

Francine considered me carefully, took a closer look at the tableau I presented, and then another look around to see if anyone was listening to us. Old habits.

"Tell me."

"He's cheating."

"Who's cheating, JK?"

"My father."

He stopped being "Dad."

"I see."

Was that the faint trace of a smile? I started to get out of my seat, but her small hand held me back with unexpected force.

"You're angry."

"Yes."

"Sad?"

"No, just angry."

"Come, let's walk."

She led me through the cemetery, keeping me close to her, my arm tucked in around hers. She listened to the whole story as we walked.

"Who is this Patrick, JK? Never mind, we'll come back to him later. So, are you quite certain about your father?"

"Certain he's a creep after all."

Wounded child speaking.

"He disappointed you,"

Francine stated the obvious. I expected more from her.

"But perhaps it isn't just that, is it, JK?"

"What?"

"Perhaps it isn't what he's doing; it's that it leaves you alone now. Just when things seemed to be turning around?"

Her keen eyes looked into mine. I turned away, walking a distance, thinking about this. Francine was right. What hurt the most was having the ground break apart under me again just when it had started to feel solid. His timing was awful. Was he only thinking of himself? Of course he was. So was I. I hadn't even given him a chance to speak last night.

I came back to her after a few minutes. She had more to say.

"Would you begrudge your father his happiness? After all your family has been through? Think about it, dear."

She patted my hand and walked away.

At a distance, she asked, "See you tomorrow?"

"Yes, tomorrow," I whispered back.

She did not need to hear my voice to know I would be there tomorrow.

I didn't visit Susie. No need to give her bad news now.

I had some thinking to do. How to parse my happiness versus his? What about Mom? And what would be on his gravestone? Imperfect husband and father?

None of it was suitable.

∞

I spent the next week at Patrick's. I grabbed some clothes from his closet and the OXFAM shop down the street. Susie would have seen right through my outfits and known something was seriously wrong, just like when it had all come to an end once before. At the start of my descent. Of course, she had been there.

Susie had been reading the menu for half an hour at our favorite café in Santa Barbara, the one we always went to when she stopped by to see me for a weekend. She was annoyed.

"Good of you to come."

I didn't respond to her sarcasm. Besides, it didn't suit her.

I was still standing, not committed to having a seat with her just yet. She looked up to see me in one of my more outlandish outfits.

"What on earth is this, JK?" Her brow knitted into deep concern. "Sit, tell me. What's wrong?"

"It's over."

I sat with a thunk in the chair opposite my bright shining sister.

"All over, Suze. You're looking at a failure."

I looked around for a waitress.

"Slow down. What are you saying?"

"They fired me. I am officially a has-been. The show is canceled, and they're not offering me a spot on any other network show. Too niche, they said. I need a drink. Where's that waitress?"

I motioned more aggressively to get some attention.

Soon I had my double vodka with a twist. Fast service, anything to stop the court jester from making a scene. The management did not know Susie would keep things in line.

"So what? You'll do something else, something better."

Susie was crestfallen but only let it show for a second, summoning all her positive energy so that she could pass it on to me. Dear Susie, she was generous that way.

"Anyway, this is a drag. I want to hear about you. Are you done yet?"

It was my favorite joke.

"JK, you know it's just the start of it. I'm one year in, still a long way to go." Susie brightened some; it was clear she loved medicine.

"And the other kids. You're all playing nice?"

It was another joke, as if she couldn't take care of herself.

"Yessss. They're a good crew. Pretty friendly, despite the competition."

That smile of hers could warm up any day of mine, that is until the time the smile was gone for good. I had to work double-duty to recover some piece of her sunshine.

∞

Dad left me multiple messages on my cell, but I didn't pick them up. I considered the situation in my very own cone of silence, and I liked the thought of being insulated.

Patrick was great. He never got into it with me. We were still "chaste," as Susie would put it, which suited me fine. He read it right; the craven thoughts were gone from my mind, replaced with a brooding morass, which was not sexy. I give Patrick credit for that time. I was not any fun.

"I'm sorry, Patrick. I know this sucks."

"It's alright, JK. You take care of your stuff, baby. I'll be here."

Baby. That one word said everything I needed to know about where he intended us to go.

For the next week, it was Francine I went to. She knew all about betrayal, the other side of the coin from mine. Yes, the woman from the cemetery was the cryptic, flawed, tragic human being that I wanted to talk to.

It was a week before I realized she was no longer the puppet master, just a woman. A genuine friend even. Maybe.

"Have you decided what you're going to do?"

"I think I have. Yes."

A week had been long enough to make up my mind.

"And?"

"I'm going back."

"Wise. Very wise." Francine continued, "I'm glad you will fight. One of us will get it right. One of us."

She still had the monkey on her back. I would come back for it. I owed her now.

$$\infty$$

Mom was back when I arrived from my talk with Francine.
"Have you met her? Jessica, I mean."

Mom asked as she busied herself placing flowers in a vase in the living room.

"Briefly."

I was thrilled to see Mom. She filled up the whole house. Even the flowers did not offend. I went straight over for a hug. Mom was a little stiff, but she hugged me right back. Even in this moment, she could not ignore the mismatched clothes on her daughter's body.

"JK. Dear? What happened to the other clothes you had?"

I just kept hugging her. Mom, so predictable!

"Well, yes. It's good to see you, too."

She pulled herself off from our hug.

"So, what do you think? Is she alright? I mean her character, of course. Can we trust her?"

Mom was anxious, almost as if she were sending her child off to camp and sizing up the camp counselor to ensure the child would be well cared for. She must have been one demanding customer with Susie and me on the line.

Wait! What did that mean? *Trust* her?

Mom kept talking, "He called me, you know. It took days before I even noticed the message. He said you were upset at the thought of it. I came home as soon as I could."

"He told you on the phone?"

This was worse than I thought.

"Mom, on the *phone*?"

"Why yes, JK. I knew something was going on, of course. A wife knows no matter what. But this . . . . Well, I have to say I had no idea of the specifics."

She looked muddled, confused even, but not hurt. Actually, she was bemused. Yes, that was the right word for it. She was bemused at her husband's infidelity.

"I would have never guessed Roger had it in him," she added cheerily. "But there you are. That man is full of surprises after all."

"Surprises? Really, Mom? Is that the word for it?"

It was my turn to be confused.

"Do you have a better word?" an arch eyebrow demanded. "He told Susie, apparently. I guess she was the only one he thought would understand. Oh, dear. It's all a mess. We have had a hard time communicating. All this lost time. "

She was off, looking at every corner of the room as if she had never inspected her own home before.

"It will be empty. The house will be empty without him. He'll be gone for a while."

It was my turn to offer support.

"It's OK, Mom. We'll figure it out."

"I know it's his turn now. But I don't want to lose him."

She had already lost him. Didn't she see that? I had to be gentle with her.

"Mom, didn't you just say Dad was going?" I asked softly.

"Yes."

"Well, doesn't that mean he'll be gone?" I continued.

"Yes." She looked at me as if I were the one that needed her help.

"JK, what's this about? You're not making much sense. Oh, Roger was right. This is difficult for you."

And just then, before I could make more of a mess, my father came out of his study with a ream of papers in one hand. He went right over to Mom.

"Patrice, Patrice darling. I'm glad you're home. I missed you so."

"Roger. Love."

And that was it. My parents were embracing! I was dumb-founded. It turned out I was deaf, blind, and dumb. Not much of an observer for a writer.

"When?" Mom asked.

"As soon as we can get the crew together, but not for another month."

"Crew? What crew?" I managed to eke out.

"JK, Ah. Err. I'm sorry you had to find out this way. I'm going to . . . ."

Dad was struggling.

"Oh Roger, it's not that difficult to say," Mom interrupted

him, her arm still around his waist.

"Your father, JK, has decided he needs to help the needy in this world. He is off to drill some wells so that those poor people can have good clean water."

She tapped his chest for emphasis. I couldn't have gotten a single sheet of paper between these two. They were holding on so tightly to each other. Bright faces looked at me.

"Not *drill* exactly, Patrice."

Ever the engineer, Dad couldn't let a detail like that pass. Of course, my enormous stupidity was another matter.

"Well, whatever it is, Roger, it's a wonderful thing, darling. See, JK. Your father is going to help people. Of course, we'll have to give him up for a while; but we'll manage, won't we?"

She was beaming and expected me to reciprocate her particular mix of smugness, pride, and sacrifice. I recognized the combination she perfected all those years while Susie and I were growing up. Roger was growing up too, it seemed.

Dad was a good man.

Mom wanted me to stay.

I had been wrong.

There it was, neatly in its box.

"Yes, we'll manage."

I had to smile back at the two of them.

"Susie, they're quite the pair, our folks. Just like us. I hear you laughing Sis. I deserve it."

∞

"I'm sorry about all of this, JK."

Dad came out to the porch, holding a beer as a peace offering. Calumet pipes were now outdated.

"May I sit?"

"It's your porch, Dad."

My sense of humor was too much for him. He was still crestfallen at our misunderstanding.

"Sure, Dad, please."

He moved slowly towards his chair and leaned in my direction. He opened his mouth to speak and closed it without a sound.

"You OK?" I asked, without making any commitments of my own.

"I am now," he said with a sigh, finally nodding and sitting back. He tried to change the topic and asked, "That fellow. Patrick, is it?"

I interrupted. "Hang on. I need to know. Who is Jessica exactly?"

"Jessica? She's my associate. She trained as an engineer, but she doesn't do the technical stuff anymore. Fundraising, logistics, staffing, that kind of thing. That's her job. I do the rest, the plans, the equipment, the project specs."

"Why didn't you tell me?"

"I was working my way to it. I was afraid of your reaction

and leaving you here alone. In case you hadn't noticed, it wasn't so easy between your mother and you."

He seemed embarrassed by that last point.

"I waited too long, I guess. I got caught out. I'm not proud of it, JK."

Dad was papa bear again. Straight and strong.

"So, nothing is going on between you two?"

"No, JK! It's your mother for me, kid. Always. That doesn't mean I don't consider Jessica a friend, just like Harry."

Boy, he was naïve! No one else would put those two in the same category. That was Dad, though. Better to leave that one alone.

"So? What about Patrick then?"

He was undeterred.

"It's good, Dad. All good."

It took me ages to say the rest of it.

"I'm sorry, Dad."

"I'm OK with you caring about what happens to this family, JK." It took Dad a while to add, "We are a family, you know."

"Not without Susie."

The words stumbled out before I could catch them.

Dad leaned over to me, firm and wise.

"JK, she's gone from our world, the world we have to live in. I wish it weren't so. I wish it had been me, but it was her. She's gone. We can only honor her with our choices. That's what she said to me when I told her about the wells: 'You honor me, Dad.' We need to do the same as she always did for us."

Damn, he had found a way forward. I wasn't there yet.

"I don't see it, Dad. I don't see it that way."

I could not leave Susie behind. Whatever salvation Dad found could not touch me.

"Alright, then," Dad sighed. "What are you going to do, JK?"

"I'm going to stick with it."

Sticky and gooey, and however else it came at me, I would do my imitation of living until maybe, someday, it wouldn't be such a fake.

Chapter 12

When Flowers Become a Good Thing

With Dad's secret in the open, the cot disappeared from the office. Mom still had flowers in the house. They didn't seem as out of place as before. We stopped tiptoeing around each other.

I still worked on writing the women's stories. It was much more complicated now. They became stubborn in their grief, same as me. Whoever tells you writing is purely intellectual is plain wrong. Any piece of work is a piece of the writer, flesh and bone. I might not have quite enough of me to go around. Still, I worked on it, hoping it would fall into place.

"JK? Are you up there?" Mom shouted from the bottom of the stairs. "Come down, dear. There's something here for you."

She almost sang the words out to me.

It was a bouquet. I knew it was from Patrick even before I opened the card. He had asked for all my contact details the day I left his apartment. Old-fashioned wooing was in play.

"And?"

"Nothing, Mom."

I smiled to myself after reading the card: Miss you making a mess of my apartment. Can we have dinner tonight and start a new mess? –P.

"I'll be out for dinner, Mom."

"I thought so."

Mom was delighted.

She came up to Susie's room later that day and sat on her bed as I combed through the wardrobe. She didn't say much; one daughter reincarnated in the other was difficult for a mother.

Her eyes glistened as she said, "You'll look marvelous, JK, whatever you pick out. Marvelous."

She left before the transformation was complete. I had not yet put on the dress. A slinky black BCBG Susie wore that night she and Jack told us about their engagement.

"Susie, it's OK, isn't it? OK, to borrow some of your happiness?"

Patrick opened the door to his place with a flourish.

"Ah, you're here. Come on in."

Patrick looked good, almost too good to wait for. But this was an old-fashioned date, so best not to tinker with the sequence of things. Once I was inside, Patrick pursued his train of thought.

"I'd tell you how good you look, but you'd just think I was thick, saying it so many times."

His eyes showed me again just what he was thinking.

JK, just savor each moment. *"Got it this time, Sis."*

"Thank you. And for the flowers. You made quite an impression on my mother."

"And her daughter too, I hope."

"Her too."

Susie as well, I was thinking. She would approve of Patrick and his ways. He had her on his side.

"Well, let's see if you're still favorably disposed after you taste the meal. It's a new recipe."

"Susie, the man cooks!"

I was in trouble. That whole week we had been together, he brought home take-out. This cooking business was new information to process—that, and how I felt about him.

Dinner was a delicious chicken tandoori.

"Easier than you might think, but you do need a charcoal grill," he said with a wink.

He was in and out of the small balcony as he cooked. He had one glass of beer out for himself and fizzy water out for me. He was thoughtful, though I expected nothing else by this time.

"Patrick, this is delicious!" I said as I tasted my first morsel.

"Hmmm, so are you."

His chocolate-brown eyes danced in the glow of the candles.

"I'm glad you like it. I didn't know how things are going back home with your folks, so I wanted you to have a treat."

"It's getting better at home."

I told him earlier on the phone I had been wrong about Dad.

He said, "At least one of us has it OK in that department."

Patrick sounded as relieved as I was.

"Better is good, isn't it?"

"For sure."

I couldn't tell him there were no absolutes. Better is relative, and that's all I had.

"Listen, let's wash up, and I can show you my collection of etchings."

I laughed out loud. This man had it all: sexiness, humor, smarts.

"You know, I am itching for some etchings right now."

He stood back in mock surprise. "Well, I started when I was young. I'm still not very good."

He jumped back when I punched him in the arm.

"Now," I said.

"Now?"

It was time we christened the bed. The sweetest nibbles led to soft kisses and then to deep, demanding kisses. His hands moved across my body, pulling me into his space and releasing me, panting a little more each time. I moaned. He sighed until I had him groaning. We repeated.

"Is this lovemaking, Susie?"

Somewhere in the middle of the night, half-asleep, I shared with Patrick my secret. "My sister, Susie, she's dead."

"I know, baby. I know."

And for the rest of the night, I let it be. Just be.

The morning came on strong as we had not thought to close the curtains. I winced in the light shining right onto my pillow.

"Patrick?"

I reached across the bed but couldn't find him.

"Patrick?"

"Yeah, babe. I'm here."

He came in from the kitchen, pants below a naked chest, the intimacy too much to bear.

"How did you know about Susie?"

I had gathered up the sheets around me.

"Your dad. He tracked me down at the bar. You gave him the name at some point. He wanted to make sure you were alright. Told me not to hurt you. You'd been through enough." Patrick stroked my cheek. "I'm sorry about your sister, JK."

My Dad was a never-ending source of surprises.

"Is that all he said?"

"All he had to say, babe."

"What did you say?"

Patrick was serious. "JK, I told your father, and now I'm telling you, it is not my intention to hurt you in any way. I'll be with you as long as you'll have me, as long as it makes sense for both of us. You get what I'm saying?"

"Why, Patrick?"

"Why does there have to be a reason, woman? It just is."

He leaned me back onto the pillows, and the sheets slipped. His pants came off quickly. We bathed in the light.

"Let it be, let it be, JK," Susie whispered. I could barely make her out.

Chapter 13

Road Trip Part 2, Sisters Revealed

Judith opened her door to Francine and me. The distance that separated her from her little sister was gone. Decades vanished.

"It's you," Judith said, as her hands fell to her side.

She wore an apron over a brown blouse with a patchy flower print and a high-waisted pair of jeans. Very Walmartish, though I wondered where she found one in this bucolic wine valley. She was slim. She tucked a strand of dull grey hair behind her ear. Her hazel eyes were alert. She wore no makeup to enhance their natural beauty. Her hands were strong but riddled with liver spots and bones jutting out for a hard edge. She wore no rings on those able hands or any jewelry other than a large translucent opal pendant hanging from her neck. It hung on a very thick but ornate gold chain and nestled itself just between her breasts. On a younger woman, it would serve as a magnet for the eyes of any interested party. I had to wonder if that had been part of its original allure for the woman. Years ago, possibly.

"It's me. Francine."

Her voice was strong, though my ear caught a slight quiver.

The two sisters looked at each other from opposite sides of the door's threshold. I saw none of Francine's pixie elegance in Judith's rugged, lived-in face. Judith had no use for makeup or showmanship, unlike Francine, who was on stage no matter how banal the setting.

Susie and I were also a mystery to those who only saw the surface of clothing and manicures. The bond between these two sisters was as palpable as Susie's and mine. Its nature, however, remained opaque. I hoped Susie and I were more wholesome, but the last few weeks had me wondering about that.

"Well, you might as well enter."

A strange turn of phrase. It might be the French showing itself. Francine's English was near perfect; her sister's was much more heavily accented.

I stood in the hallway after Francine entered, waiting to be invited.

"You, too, young lady."

There, finally. The expression I heard from Francine for weeks. The concrete sign of a connection.

"This is JK," announced Francine. "She has been a good friend to me recently. She drove me here."

As if getting in a car signaled an incredibly intimate relationship. I still knew very little about Francine. I expected much from this visit.

"So."

"So."

The two circled each other, each waiting for a move from the other. Careful now. This scene was not yet choreographed. I wasn't the writer; these two sisters were.

"How unoriginal we've become." It was Judith who spoke. Francine simply nodded.

"I suppose I should offer you some coffee?"

"That would be nice."

I had to say something. "Need some help?"

"Certainly, young lady. This way."

I followed the upright elderly lady (she had to be in her late seventies) into a small galley kitchen. The place was spotless. Clean, but old. The countertop Formica was burned in a few spots and curled up on one corner as if it knew it had been too long in this world, and it was time to get up and go. I doubted there would be any kind of renovation unless a clamor went up from every resident all at once. And that would not happen anytime soon.

Judith reached into a cupboard for an old tin can. Her hands smoothed over its surface. She wasn't yet ready to open it. With one hand on the counter for support, she handed me the tin.

"This has traveled with me quite some distance with me.

'Quite a ways' you Americans would say. Many memories. Now it holds coffee. Here. You open it."

The misshapen tin was a challenge to open. I finally managed to pry the top off and handed it back to the older woman.

"Here you go."

"Oh. Thank you. The thing is impossible to open."

She was staring into the drain of the kitchen sink.

"Would you reach over to the coffee maker, please? A full pot would do nicely. Up there in the left-most cabinet."

A pungent aroma wafted into the tiny kitchen. My stomach growled audibly.

Judith was a gracious hostess.

"Oh, I suppose you will need something to eat with the coffee. Here, I have some scones. I make them every Monday for the start of the week. You're in luck; they're still fresh."

"That would be great."

"I will leave you to it. Join us when you're ready."

And with that, she left to join her sister in the other room. OK, not so gracious.

I looked around, trying to decide where the scones might be. It took a short while before I located them in the fridge. The coffee pot took some time to figure out. Judith must be a tea drinker, I thought; nobody had used the pot in some time. I decided to clean it out thoroughly before setting it up for brewing.

Finally, with the coffee pot on a tray with three mugs, I

made my way into the room where the two sisters sat at the edge of the tattered sofa.

"Oh, and some sugar please, JK?" asked Judith, looking up at me, trying to shoo me away.

Cleaning the pot had not chewed up enough time for her.

It was not the time to ask how to prepare the scones. Instead, I would toast them, a trick I had learned from that young British actress on a show. While I watched the toaster oven glow red, I marveled at how quickly Judith pushed me out of the sisters' world, relegating me to serving.

Sugar and warm scones in hand, I returned to them and sat down in the armchair opposite the pair. Finally, the triangle was complete, and I was free to observe the sisters' sparring exchange.

"Have you been back?" Judith asked her younger sister.

"Yes, we went back once." Francine closed her eyes as she spoke.

"Ah, so it's true."

"He did find me. That much is true."

"I never went back. Came to America with a young GI. I left him quite quickly. Men were never my thing after France."

"So, all these years, you've been . . . ?"

"Alone. My work, of course. But no one else."

"Your work?"

"Nursing. I became a nurse after the war."

"That makes sense. You were always interested in medicine."

"You remember. I wanted to be a doctor back then. It didn't quite turn out as I once thought, but there it is. I managed. Better than many."

The conversation halted. Francine sized up the place inch by inch at record speed. Satisfied with her view of her sister's dim life, Francine reached for a scone.

"Are these from Maman's recipe?"

"Yes, same as hers. I bake once a week. It's been my only connection. Well, until now." A dash of impatience, "Why are you here, Francine?"

Why indeed, I wondered. There was no warmth between the two women. I munched into the scone, washed it down with the delicious coffee, and waited for what would come next. We were there for an hour; that was all the time needed to pull the air out from between these two sisters.

When Francine and I walked out of the building, Bill waved at us, his wise, wrinkled face nodding. I stopped to speak with him for a moment while Francine walked on to the car.

"Did Judith treat you right?" he asked me.

"How'd you know?" I asked.

"The kid at the desk can't keep his mouth shut," Bill replied. "So, was it what you expected?"

"Me? I didn't know what to expect." I was truthful. "For her," I pointed to Francine, who was standing pert by her side of the car, "I think it was worse. Much worse than she expected."

"Can't say I'm surprised. No sir. The likes of her, always to be disappointed, I reckon."

Just then, Francine came back from the car. "JK, stay here if you would. I'd like to head back in. Just for a moment."

She didn't wait for an answer.

"Well then. What do you think that's all about?" Bill was thinking out loud, waiting for me to respond.

"Dunno. Maybe she needs to make amends? Or maybe it's another grenade. Honestly, I just don't know."

I was spent. The drama of it all was more than a one-hour TV show. That was my limit, after all.

"Here, kid, you sit here with me." Bill patted the bench next to him.

I sat with the old man. He rambled on some. I listened. He had been in the war and came back to see his girl snatched up by some business type who had a "medical condition" barring him from service. Lucky for Bill, he later met his lovely wife Chantra at church. They had been happy together and blessed. His kids and grandkids came every week. He was a happy man. Would have liked Chantra with him, he said. She had been gone five years now. That was his only regret. Sigh. Smile.

"Does it get any easier, Bill?"

"Nope, it just gets more real. Each day, she's more gone."

Bill's face was a puzzle. My own reflected upon his, I suppose.

"Wish I could tell you otherwise."

Had I never noticed there was a screenplay around every corner? There was something deceptively simple in Bill's recounting of his life.

When Francine came out the second time, she walked briskly, clutching her purse more protectively than before.

"You ladies take care now."

Bill's voice conveyed more warmth than we deserved.

"You too, Bill." I impulsively leaned into him for a hug. "You, too."

"Will do, kid."

I walked back to the car. We were both seated and ready to head back when something told me to pause. I might not know everything there was to know yet. I took a deep breath and turned to Francine.

"What happened?" I asked.

To my surprise, Francine didn't hesitate to describe what happened with her sister while I had been waiting outside with Bill. Her retelling transported me to their scene as if I had been there.

"Why are you here, Francine?"

Judith's speech had been crisp before. Now she was downright hostile.

"I came to speak with you. Things are not done."

Francine played it straight, no sugar added.

"Really? After all this time? You want something, don't you?"

Judith was weary.

"He's dead, you know," Francine added, for good measure. "He died."

Judith's hand went to the pendant. "When?"

"A few months ago."

"How?" Judith appeared suspicious.

"Does it matter?"

Francine was deadpan.

Judith considered her sister.

"I suppose it doesn't. How long?"

"We were together fifty years. Long years."

Francine's eyes dimmed as she told me about telling Judith it had been fifty years. She told me she was thinking of all the years she had thrown away.

"We lived in the States. Somehow, he managed that much. He was quite capable, you know. I did convince him to let me dance. He was a jealous sort, so it didn't last long, but I had that piece of me for a while. Small victories, you know."

"Judith, he had been so powerful, at first. It was difficult for him to be reduced. He took it out on those around him. Rather unpleasant."

As Francine told me of her conversation with Judith, she smoothed her skirt, as I had seen her do many times, like she wanted to push away troubling thoughts.

"Isn't that ironic," Judith said.

"Judith, please, I was a child."

"You! You were never innocent, Francine."

Francine told me Judith's anger cut through the air, and she stood up in a rush and left the room. That was the end of the exchange, according to Francine.

She looked at me miserably. I felt the unexpected burden of having to say something. I resorted to a benign query: "Your sister? How long has it been?"

"Oh, I don't know. At least fifty-five years." A quizzical look crossed my face. The game was back on.

I lost all patience. "Francine, would you just tell me what happened?"

"What happened?"

"Between you and your sister?"

"Rivalry of a sort, JK. A silly game I started and didn't know how to end. I was a child."

Francine repeated her mantra. It was no more convincing to me than she said it had been to Judith.

"Francine, you're not being straight with me."

"With you or with anyone, JK. My life has been an act. Sad but true. It was the only way to survive all those years with Franz. Never showed my true feelings."

Francine was rock hard.

"I hated him."

"Why did you marry someone you hated?"

"It was my penance. Oh, at first, I didn't see it that way. He still cut a dashing figure. I suppose there was something sexual to it."

Francine waved her hand in the air as if to dismiss the

thought.

"But even that was a disappointment in time."

"I don't understand."

"You live in another world." Francine patted my hand.

"Could I ask you to go back to my sister for me? Please. I can't stand to leave it this way."

She had a chance with her sister. I, the one who did not have a chance with mine, decided I would go to Judith.

As I headed back in to mediate peace with Judith, I realized Francine had deflected my question. She spoke of her husband but not of what had brought her to her sister. The young man at the desk did not make eye contact, and I did not offer any niceties. I was on a mission.

The door to the apartment was unlocked, and I went in.

"Judith?" I walked past the kitchen down a hallway to what I thought would be the bedroom. I knocked on the half-open door. "Judith? It's JK. Are you here?"

"Yes." A soft voice answered.

I pushed the door open fully and saw a time capsule: an old-fashioned bedroom set, a sleigh bed in dark wood, a matching boudoir set, a chaise and a mirror, some old black-and-white photographs on the dresser. Time was trapped in the room. Judith was both keeper and prisoner.

I went over to her and sat on the bed. It was an unusually soft mattress, and I slipped against her. Then, as I pushed back clumsily, I said, "I'm so sorry. Did I hurt you?"

"It's been so long since someone touched me." Judith bounded up. "No, you did not hurt me, JK."

She walked over to the dresser and picked up one of the framed pictures. Two little girls, doubtless the two sisters of long ago.

"We were happy once." Sigh. Judith looked back at me from a world long ago. "How I live seems sad to you, no?"

"Sad? I don't know that that's the word. Disconnected, maybe?"

"Disconnected. Yes, you could be right. I had to leave it all behind. But the past won't let me go. And now . . . ." Judith still held on to the pendant and saw me admiring it.

"Do you like it?"

"It's stunning."

"It belonged to my mother. Unfortunately, she died during the war."

"Francine told me."

"Did she tell you how?"

"We never got that far."

"I see. My mother died of a broken heart. Our father went to fight and never returned. It was as if the air was pulled out of Maman's lungs. The last straw was when the Germans took over the village. Franz, he was their captain. He took over our house. Took it all."

Judith was pained. Her grief was as real as in the moment when it happened years ago.

"Remember, JK. You must go on," I remember Susie said to me.

"Sis, I know you said that. Don't you think I'm trying?"

"Try harder, JK. Harder."

I shut my eyes as Judith continued.

"It wasn't long before he made himself clear. Francine and I could have anything we wanted. Meat, cheese, fresh fruits and vegetables, even medicine, all in exchange for certain favors." Judith stopped there.

I was shocked, even though somewhere in my mind I had expected this.

"Francine, she was, well, she was young, but not so young. He looked at her, too."

"You mean?"

"Yes. He had no sense of courtesy if that's the correct word."

Judith pursed her mouth the same way her sister did at the cemetery.

"There was the question of food and then also of my sister and how best to protect her. I had nowhere to turn."

"So, you . . . .?"

"I did. He was kindly, at first. Gentle. But I never kissed him. Never!"

She was defiant now and must have been with the German officer too. Perhaps that excited him more. "Then . . . ."

"Not so gentle," I finished for her.

It was a fact out of time, hardly much to guess at.

"No, not gentle at all."

She rubbed her arms across her chest, flattening her breasts, wishing them away.

She continued sadly, "Not so unusual a story for wartime, is it?"

Judith went on, her terrible secret about to burst.

"I'm sorry; you can't even imagine what it was like. Famine, disease, death all around. Betrayal. Francine was young too. But as I said, not so young. She started to get jealous. She started to provoke him. It was silly at first, a naïve girl trying to attract a man like that. But she had a . . . a certain talent, shall we say. I became worried. You see, he was quite an imaginative man."

A shadow passed over Judith. I could see her as a young girl, trapped in an impossible situation.

"I begged him to keep her out of it. I did everything he asked. I was his whore. All for her. All for her."

Youth slipped away. Judith was back in the weathered place she now lived in. "It went on several years. The shame of it. I still feel his breath on me, even now, an old lady."

"I'm so sorry, Judith."

Weak words meant to soothe were all I could muster.

Judith bravely continued. "At the end of the war, I had to flee. No one in the village would forgive me. I still wonder how they found out what happened in the house. We were very discreet."

She was back, self-possessed.

"You do understand my meaning, JK? I do not wish to know how it was discovered."

"Give this to her. Go now, please." Judith gave me the framed picture. "Take this with you. Say . . . just say goodbye."

I stared at the innocent girls in the picture frame. They were frozen at that moment, arms carelessly draped one around the other, their whole lives ahead of them.

Chapter 14

The Professor and the Book

Spring livened my walk through the university campus. I registered the hustle of activity and pheromones as I strolled to my old haunt, Wheeler Hall. Berkeley was humming with the rushing about of the young ones. I was older now, and my pace reflected the accumulated years.

"JK, it's been a while!"

The Professor's face lit up with genuine pleasure. Professor Smithfield was just as I remembered him: kindly, a little sloppy in his dress, and fully engaged from the moment I stepped into his office.

"Please sit, JK. You surprised me, you know."

"Hello there, Professor."

I grinned. I felt alive, back on familiar territory.

"I was pleased to get a copy of your most recent work. Thank you for sending it."

He patted the thick bunch of papers of the women's stories I mailed him a month earlier, requesting his opinion.

I had finally managed to bring my book together over the past months between seeing Dad off to go to the wells, sticking it out with Mom, and seeing more of Patrick. The winter was not too cold, so I still walked with Francine through the cemetery. But neither of us broached the story of the French sisters. Susie was a constant in my life.

"What do you think?" I asked the professor.

"What do *you* think, JK?"

"Uh, dunno really. It's different for me."

"It certainly is."

He folded his reading glasses and leaned over the desk somewhat protectively over the papers.

"May I ask where the inspiration came from?"

"It's from . . . ."

I found I could not share with the professor the truth of the past months.

"I can't say."

"I see. Well, never mind that."

He hid his disappointment well.

"It's quite a piece, JK. Intimate, wretched. Yet cold, calculating. Quite unlike your previous work. You're more passionate than this, I think."

"So, you don't like it?"

I was sunk.

"Did I say that? No, my dear. I believe it is a good piece.

One which no doubt could have quite a bit of success. But it's not you, at least not the JK I know."

"Professor, I don't understand."

"Let me explain. I was taken all those years ago by your fragility, your grit, the sheer aggression of your words. You were courageous, clear, razor-sharp in your writing. It leaped off the page straight into a person's heart."

"So, this doesn't touch you?"

"It does, JK, but it touches the mind, not the heart. You withheld the most important ingredient: your own heart."

He patted his chest, reading glasses hanging off his thumb.

"I see."

"It's not you."

He had a habit of repeating himself.

Really, not me? Who was I but an accumulation of false starts and half promises? Only half without Susie, great big pieces of me gone with her.

"Susie, of course, I'll go on," I told her at the end. Lying on the starched, scratchy linens of the hospital bed, she was small, barely a fraction of herself. Susie was slipping. Her weak hand in mine, eyes fixed somewhere beyond me. She could barely speak.

Goodbyes to Mom and Dad moved them to the corner of the room while I had my moment. My last moment with Susie.

"Promise me, JK. Promise you'll go on." The croak of her voice filled that room and my ears for all time.

"I will, Sis. Of course, I will."

Did I sound as convincing as she needed me to be?

"JK?"

"Yes?"

"I was lucky. Lucky to have you."

"I was a pain, Suze. I'm sorry."

My tears spilled onto her.

"No, you were there. Always there. My lovely, lovely sister." Her voice was gentle.

"I'm cold, JK."

"Hang on, Susie."

I got into bed and pulled the blanket over us. Full circle, back in the womb. Susie exited first, just like she did when we were born. I would follow. Later. After. Once I figured out how to live without her.

"Not me?" I asked the professor angrily, more terse than the gentleman deserved from me. "A person can change, can't they?"

The professor came back at me softly. "I was sorry to hear about your difficulties, my dear. And, of course, the death of your sister."

"You know?"

The anger left as suddenly as it had arrived.

"Well, I was so surprised when I read the piece you sent me that I did a bit of research. You'll forgive me, no?"

He afforded me some measure of control.

"Of course I do, Professor. I'm just not clear on what to do next."

Emptiness ahead.

"Well, if you'll allow me, I have a suggestion."

"Sure, why not?" Then with more kindliness from me, "I would like that very much. Professor."

He explained himself. His idea laid a path I could follow.

"Susie, I know you're lighting the way."

I could hear my sister saying, "No, JK, this is you and the people who care about you."

Chapter 15

Laying Bare

M om dragged me back. No, that's not exactly true. She suggested; I said yes. I had been writing about the women for so long. Could I shy away from facing them?

The room was barer than I remembered. Clinical. I headed into the circle with only a scuffed-up chair for support.

"Hi, I'm JK. It stands for Josephine Kelly, but I prefer JK."

"Hi, JK," their many voices responded, not quite in unison.

"I lost my sister, Susie. She was my twin. Well, not exactly lost. She wasn't a puppy without a leash."

Fragile smiles told me they understood the reason for my weak attempt at humor. Little girl, it's alright; go on now.

"Susie, she left a lot behind. Mostly a big hole, negative space. You know?"

They knew.

"The memories, even the good, happy memories, they're

fading. I can't hang on to her. She did everything for me. She saved me. But I couldn't . . . ."

"Shush, Susie. You know it's true. I failed you."

So sorry, the same genuine words, unspoken this time. The women had been through their separate versions of loss. We owned our grief, cherished it even. If it stayed with us, so did Susie, Richard, Billy, and all of them. They would stay.

"Stay with me, Susie."

Look at these women around you, JK.

The women were luminous, driven by desire. Incandescent madness. No, terrible emptiness. That's it. Emptiness. Void. Nothing. The women started to talk, the same voices I had for company while writing about them. They went round and round.

Get off the merry-go-round, JK. Go forward. It was time to honor Susie's last request. Honor her for all she had been to me.

I stood up to go before time was up. One of the mothers looked up at me. I thought, for a second, she would move, too. But it wasn't her time yet. I left alone.

Mom waited outside for me.

"Why weren't you in there, Mom?"

"These things are private, dear. I thought you'd find it easier without me."

The professor was right; I had a lot more to say about the women. It would take time. A heck of a lot of time.

"Let's go, Mom. I know a great ice cream parlor."

"Alright, dear. Just give me a moment; then I'll be with you."

I watched the complex, difficult, lovely Patrice, wife, and mother head into the ladies' room to pull herself together before she could face the world.

Mom said she didn't want any ice cream, but Pearl served us each a scoop with that same sure hand on my mother's shoulder.

"A lady can change her mind," Pearl said.

Mom and I talked about her new plans for the garden. Spring was the time to plant, she said. We would then have flowers in the house all year round without having to help the florist buy a boat. She seemed pleased with her greening projects. She asked about Patrick. Even though I didn't say much, I knew the smile on my face told the story.

Pearl nodded to herself when she cleared our table.

"You come back soon, ladies."

We had both finished our scoops. No spoons left unused this time.

It was a new split out of time, one I hoped Mom and I would repeat. Mother and daughter straight out of a TV scene, but this time in real life.

Chapter 16

Pieced Together

"You're leaving? Where are you going?" Mom was startled by my announcement. "But things are going so well!" Mom and I had reached equilibrium without Dad over the past months. She returned to her old ways; I was more forgiving of them. She tried hard to respect my choices. Of course, it helped that she liked Patrick right away. "Don't lose him, dear."

"I'll wait until Dad comes home before I leave, of course."

Our video Skype calls from India revealed him in his glory. Yes, things were going well with the project. He answered every time we called, even though it was either late or early for him, given the time difference. He was out there doing what he promised himself and Susie he would do.

I was proud of him, and Mom positively beamed every time she spoke of him. He was due home in a couple of weeks. They would be fine now. My folks, they'd be just fine. Check one.

"Well, I don't know what to say. I suppose it's for the best." Mom bit her lip. "You'll visit, of course. Maybe we'll fly out to see you, too. New York is still part of this continent last time I checked. That's right. We will come to see you."

She brightened some at that thought.

"What about Patrick? He is such a nice young man."

She clouded over at the thought.

"We've talked. It's the right move for me. He understands."

I couldn't tell Mom yet that Patrick was thinking of moving out as well, closer to the two women he loved. Wink. Smile. We would see on that front. I was through rushing ahead. Patience was a new virtue of mine.

"So, this job. Is it, you know, secure?" Mom spoke this last word softly.

"Nothing is secure these days, Mom. But I think it's solid. It will do me fine for now."

The professor had made introductions to a publishing firm in New York. It turned out they liked my critical eye for the new youth literature, as they called it, all that edgy stuff that was so popular. Prof suggested leaving the women's stories to one side. His idea was to take the experience in New York and, in a few months, come back to my book and put more of myself into it.

"You'll see, JK. The heart will come and make the book better."

All things are relative, Professor.

I smiled at Mom. I was getting myself onto a straightaway

after a long haul down the winding road of confusing traffic signals.

I had one more person to tell.

"Francine!" I shouted over to her. "Here, I'm here."

Not for long. I ran over to her.

"JK, I'm glad to see you. I have something to tell you."

"Me, too."

We both took in this moment. It had been six months since we first met each other. Time had moved on since then, and I finally had caught up. In our recent walks, she had been good at listening to the women's stories I was writing.

And, of course, she had been delighted to hear more about Patrick.

"He sounds just wonderful, my dear."

"I'm leaving, heading to New York."

"Oh my. I'm leaving, too. How extraordinary!"

Francine fretted some. I decided to go all in.

"So, I think it's time you told me the truth of it."

"Truth?"

"Yes."

Firm but gentle now, I waited for my answers. They were for her I told myself. I owed her. Monkey, Monkey, that's not your place, come off her. I was determined to help.

"You want to know about that time, don't you?"

She sighed, a soft sound almost as if all she was doing was flicking off a speck of dust from her shoulder.

"Very well, young JK, you shall have your truth."

I winced at the choice of words. Clever Francine was on the stage.

"You'll remember the Germans came to our house. Mother died. A broken heart, I suspect. I think Judith would have agreed with me on this point. Correct?"

I nodded.

"Judith, well, she did certain things. We never spoke directly about it, not then and not recently either. But I knew. I knew she was sleeping with the German officer. Smart really. Always go with the top man if you can, I suppose. Clever Judith until she was clever no more."

Francine stopped. She held Susie's shawl tight, too tight.

"Francine?"

"Oh, yes, where was I? They thought they were discreet, but I knew. The first time I heard those noises from the living room, I ran down the stairs, straight to the kitchen for a knife, the biggest one I could find. He had Judith on the couch and was stroking her leg. No need for the knife. Judith did not resist. I went back to my room, sick to my stomach but also pleased in some way. It was arousing."

Francine looked at me. "Are you shocked, JK?"

"No, surprised maybe."

Surprised you're honest about this, Francine. Perhaps there

is truth in you yet.

"Well, it went on and on, for years. I watched them. It was sick. I saw what he did. She submitted, submitted to it all. I finally understood how badly he used her. I kept watching. I didn't want her to be alone. Finally, there was no more arousal; I was sick of it."

Francine sobbed once. "I couldn't leave her alone. Do you understand me, JK? Do you?"

"But you never spoke to her about it?"

"No. I told you, we never spoke of it. She would have been devastated if she knew I knew. I couldn't add to her burden. No."

"So, you did nothing to help?"

"JK, she was my sister. Of course, I tried to help! I did everything I could do to entice him so she wouldn't bear it alone. He must have been too captivated with her; it didn't work. I tried even harder, but I was not successful. Perhaps I was too young for him."

Oh, how contrived love is! Each sister trying to save the other, misunderstanding intent. Where was Shakespeare? This was a tragedy. They had misled each other and themselves.

"It wasn't me, you know. It wasn't me who turned her in."

Francine was defiant.

"Who then?"

"I never knew how it got out. Maybe the doctor she went to see? Maybe a jealous neighbor? No one would answer my questions. I left the village. There was nothing for me after Judith was banished that way."

Francine, little one, alone. No wonder she was tough as nails. How else would she survive?

"And you already know the rest. Franz found me at my aunt's in Brittany several years after the war. My aunt was hateful to me, an angry old witch. Franz, well, he somehow turned himself into a Polish refugee. He promised me a better life. He had money stashed away. His wife did not survive the liberation of Berlin, he told me. Was it true? Who knows? And Judith? That's where he was most ruthless."

"Oh, your sister. Do you want to go over that old ground again?" Franz asked me. "I know you liked watching us. Maybe I can find her now and start again? Or should it be you? Time to get into the picture, Francine. Yes, it's your turn now."

Francine stood stiffly. "You see, JK, I was finally old enough for him. No longer a little girl for a thirty-year-old officer, I was twenty-one by then and ripe."

"Was it a bad marriage?"

"Bad? Oh, I don't know. The war in a sense defeated him, and I was prepared for him. But still, it wasn't long before I wanted to kill him. But don't most women wish their husbands dead at some point?"

There was a dark look in her eye. Francine was moving past her own story into her present-day personage.

I had just started to breathe more easily when her final zinger came at me.

"It's a loss, JK. It's a bigger loss to lose who you hate than who you love. I found I had no feelings at all when he died.

None, until you came."

"Until I came? Me?"

"Yes, you, my dear. You were lost, so unhappy. I felt sorry for you at first."

Francine patted me. Affection?

"Then, I grew to admire you. You fought the loss of your sister valiantly. Quite the little warrior."

Like Mom, I was a warrior.

"In fact, it's because of you I went to see Judith. I thought I could also fight for my sister."

"Can I ask you something?"

"Of course, JK, you may ask anything you wish."

"What did you say to Judith when you went back in to see her alone?" I asked. "You never told me the whole story."

"Say? Just like back then. Nothing to say. She tried to give me the picture of us, from before the war. I told her to keep it. She'd had it all those years and would be lonely without it."

"What about you?"

"Me? I was not thinking about myself at that moment. And then she sent you back out with the picture. So we never did get aligned."

Francine dropped her head in sorrow for the first and only time since I had known her.

I felt myself genuinely connected to Francine. I still couldn't tell if her story was a clever twist on what I had told her about the conversation I had with Judith. All I knew for sure was that somewhere in her mind, she created pieces of memories where she had tried to be a good sister.

A week later, Francine and I were in her hotel room for a final goodbye. She told me on the phone that Franz's probate had finally been released with the cause of death deemed to be "accidental overdose of Warfarin." Franz bled out copiously and painfully, all because of a miscalculation in that rat poison of a medicine. She was free to go, the money would now follow.

I sat on her bed as she busied herself with the last of her packing. She looked at her reflection in the mirror for a while. Was she recalling her past beauty, the youthful dreams I saw in the picture from Judith? Finally, she took in her image one last time and turned from the mirror to me.

"Was I unfair to you, JK? You had been through a lot and so young. Anyone visiting a cemetery is recoiling from life."

She continued after a brief pause. "If I was unfair, I don't regret it. You were so eager for my story. And it didn't disappoint you, did it?"

I didn't answer. My interest in her had grown well beyond simple curiosity.

"Well, JK, you've had the truth." She spoke softly now. "Almost all of it."

In the next minute, I understood much more about Francine.

"A dancer can't be expected to be a nurse, can she?"

After a dramatic pause, she continued, "The manner of his death seemed fitting to me. Too bad he had not been prescribed that medicine earlier; I might have had more good years. Never mind. Look ahead, JK. Look forward."

I should have guessed. This woman was not a victim, she had chosen her path.

"Judith and I can be comfortable now. At last."

She looked into my eyes as she said, "That's all for now, JK. You stay here. I have a ride arranged."

She held my arm one last time before she turned from me. Even the fiercest need to speak their truths out loud, no matter the horror. And so it was that I came to understand my role in my relationship with Francine.

Having completed her confession, Francine dismissed me. She walked out of the shabby room like she was exiting the stage. She closed this chapter of the book. The door shut firmly behind her.

Her step was lighter than I had seen in the past in the cemetery.

Her shoes were clean. Her hands were another matter.

A beautiful black cashmere wrap was draped on the hotel bed. I picked it up and breathed in the complicated perfume.

∞

"Hey, Susie. I'm heading out. I got a gig in New York with a publishing house. They like my talent for spotting edgy authors."

"I hear you, Sis. About time. I know."

"Dad is, well, he's a little sad. But, hey, you know that project with the wells? Yes, the small children in India and all of that. He's a got a partner too. Nice lady. The first trip was a raging success. Good old Dad."

"Mom? Well, she came home. I think she may be getting out of her dark place. It comes and goes, you know. She's not permanently stuck there. I guess that's good, right? I saw her, though, Susie. I did, she was a real person. Then she went back into her armor. Maybe it's the only way she has to keep going. I think that's it, you know? It's her only way."

"Patrick? He's fine. He said he'd come out east for a while. So we'll see what happens."

I had never spoken to Susie about Francine. No need to start now.

"So, Sis. I should ask you to be good up there. But that is like telling an angel to stay close to the big guy."

"I miss you, Susie."

Later. "I'm sorry, Susie."

Much later. "I love you, Susie. You're the best."

Last. "You fought a good fight, Susie. It's my turn now."

∞

The sun was already coming down as I left the cemetery for the airport where a giant metal bird would wing me off to my next stop.

Patrick was waiting at the gate. He was my escort all the way to New York.

"Is everything alright?" he asked.

I told him I was pieces of myself. The only time I recognized them was when they crashed into pieces of Susie. So, I would keep her with me.

Acknowledgments

To my dear friends, thank you for your encouragement, thoughtfulness, and enthusiasm. To my colleagues who waited until I retired to publish, I hope your patience was rewarded. To my family, you're always close to my heart and never far from my thoughts. To the team at Dreams Accelerator, I am grateful you improved the book. And last, to my husband Ed, I was lucky your real estate search brought you to my door. Thank you for being so open and loving about all things in our lives, including my writing projects.

Writing a book is an act of faith. Faith in oneself, Faith in the process, Faith from loved ones. I was lucky on all counts. A one-year hiatus in between jobs provided me the space and time to explore this passion. Being an avid reader is not the same as producing a story and characters that people will care about. I discovered I could do it, and better yet, that I loved it.

JK's voice rang loud and clear in my mind as I wrote. I hope pieces of her will remain with you as they do with me.

About the Author

Névine Zariffa, author of *Sisters Pieced Together*, believes the richest life is lived at the intersection of thinking and feeling. She says she cannot imagine anything more deeply human than writing.

Her family immigrated to Montréal from Egypt when she was a baby. In her early 30's, she faced the dire diagnosis of leukemia. Luckily, a new treatment was discovered in time, and her life became hers to live. She is married to a man she declares to be wonderful. They enjoy being with their friends and family, especially their grandchildren. They consider both Montréal and Philadelphia as home.

Prior to writing *Sisters Pieced Together*, Névine enjoyed a fulfilling twenty-five year career developing new medicines for patients, as others had for her. She is the Founder of NMD Group, a strategic consulting firm dedicated to advancing healthcare. Her clients include the US FDA, Friends of Cancer Research, and the Bill and Melinda Gates Foundation. She is also on the executive leadership team of a worldwide data research lab addressing COVID-19.

She is delighted to be able to devote time to writing while working for patients through her ongoing professional activities.

For more, visit www.NevineZariffa.com.

Made in the USA
Middletown, DE
25 September 2023

39371313R00106